The Door Was Yanked Open Suddenly And There She Stood.

Even in her worn jeans and button-down white shirt, she took his damn breath away and he resented that fact down to his bones.

Distance hadn't helped. He'd thought of her. Dreamed of her, and awakened nearly every morning with his body tight and ready for her.

Even now, the lush, slightly floral scent of her reached out to him as if to tease every sense memory he had of touching her, tasting her, being inside her....

Jaw tight, he looked deeply into those calm blue eyes and wondered if she was as unaffected by him as she seemed.

Dear Reader,

I love Ireland. It's my favorite place to visit, and every time I go, it's harder and harder to leave. Everything about that country appeals to me, from the staggering beauty of the countryside to the bustle of the cities and especially the warmth of its people.

So writing this story was really fun for me. Ronan Connolly lives in Ireland, but he's in California on business. His life gets complicated, though, when he meets Laura Page.

Sweeping her off to Ireland for a romantic visit is, Ronan thinks, the way to get her out of his system. But Laura isn't the kind of woman it's easy to walk away from. Soon enough, he realizes he doesn't *want* to lose her. The problem is finding a way to keep her without engaging his heart.

I hope you enjoy *Up Close and Personal* as much as I did.

You can visit me on Facebook, Twitter and at my website, www.maureenchild.com.

I wish you all great books and the time to relish them.

Maureen

MAUREEN CHILD

UP CLOSE AND PERSONAL

HARLEQUIN®
entertain, enrich, inspire™

ISBN-13: 978-0-373-73192-3

UP CLOSE AND PERSONAL

Books by Maureen Child

Harlequin Desire

Silhouette Desire

†Reasons for Revenge
*Kings of California

Other titles by this author available in ebook format.

MAUREEN CHILD

is a California native who loves to travel. Every chance they get, she and her husband are taking off on another research trip. An author of more than sixty books, Maureen loves a happy ending and still swears that she has the best job in the world. She lives in Southern California with her husband, two children and a golden retriever with delusions of grandeur. Visit Maureen's website, www.maureenchild.com.

For Patti Hambleton
That first trip to Ireland was the best
Because it was shared with you.
For all the years, for all the laughs,
I love you, my friend.

One

"Laura, I know you're in there!"

Ronan Connolly pounded on the brightly painted blue front door a few more times, then paused to listen. Not a sound from inside the house, though he knew too well that Laura was in there. Hell, he could practically *feel* her, standing just on the other side of the damned door.

Bloody hardheaded woman. How had he ever thought that quality attractive? Now that attractive hardheadedness had come back to bite him in the ass.

Seconds ticked past and there was no sound from within, which only irritated him further. He glanced at the sunshine-yellow Volkswagen parked alongside the house—her car—then glared again at the still-closed front door.

"You won't convince me you're not at home. Your bloody car is parked in the street, Laura."

Her voice came then, muffled but clear. "It's a driveway in America, Ronan. You're not in Ireland, remember?"

"More's the pity." He scrubbed one hand across his face and rolled his eyes in frustration. If they were in Ireland right now, he'd have half the village of Dunley on his side and he'd bloody well get her to open the damned door.

"I heard that," she said. "And feel free to hop onto one of your private planes and go back to Connolly-land anytime you feel like it!"

If only he could, Ronan thought. But he'd come to California to open an American branch of his business and until Cosain was running as it should, he was going nowhere at all.

At the moment though, he was tired, on edge and in no mood to be dealing with more females. Especially one with a head as hard as Laura's.

He had spent the past six weeks traveling across Europe acting as bodyguard to a sixteen-year-old pop star whose singing was only slightly less annoying than her attitude. Between the girl and her grasping mother, Ronan had been more than ready for the job to end so he could get back to his life. Now that he was back, he'd expected peace. Orderliness. Instead...

Grinding his teeth together, he took a long moment or two and counted to ten. Then did it a second time. "Whatever the hell you want to call it, Laura, your car is *here* and so're you."

"I might have been out," she shouted. "Did you ever think of that? I do have friends, you know."

The Connolly temper lifted a couple notches inside him and Ronan was forced to fight it back down.

"But you're not out, are you?" he asked, entirely reasonably, and he gave himself points for it. "You're here, driving me to distraction and making me shout at a bloody closed door like I'm the village idiot turned loose on his own for the first time."

"You don't have to shout, I can hear you," she said, her voice carrying nicely through the door.

Laura Page lived on a tidy street in Huntington Beach, California, in one of a dozen town houses built to look like a Cape Cod village. When he'd first seen her place, he'd thought it charming. Now he glared at the building as if it were to blame for his current situation.

A cool ocean breeze shot down the narrow street and rattled the limbs of the nearly naked elm tree in Laura's front yard. Roiling gray clouds overhead promised a storm soon, and he hoped to hell he wasn't still standing on this bleeding porch when it hit.

"Your neighbors can hear me, too," he pointed out with a brief nod at the man clipping his hedge with enough vigor to whittle it into a toothpick. "Why not open the door and we can talk this out. Together. In private."

"I've got nothing to say to you."

He laughed shortly. That would be a first indeed, he told himself. A more opinionated woman he had never met. In the beginning, he'd liked that about her. Too often, he was surrounded by smiling, vacuous women who agreed with everything he said and laughed at the lamest of jokes just to ingratiate themselves with him.

But not Laura.

No, from the first, she had been stubborn and argumentative and unimpressed with his wealth or celebrity. He had to admit, he had enjoyed verbally sparring with her. He admired a quick mind and a sharp tongue. He'd admired her even more once he'd gotten her into his bed.

He glanced down at the dozen red roses he held

clutched in his right hand and called himself a damned fool for thinking this woman would be swayed by pretty flowers and a smooth speech. Hell, she hadn't even *seen* the flowers yet. And at this rate, she never would.

Huffing out an impatient breath, he lowered his voice a bit. "You know why I'm here. Let's get it done and have it over then."

There was a moment's pause, as if she were thinking about what he'd said. Then she spoke up again. "You can't have him."

"What?"

"You heard me," she called back and Ronan narrowed his gaze fiercely on the door as if he could see through the panel to the woman beyond.

"Aye, I heard you. Though I don't believe it. I've come for what's mine, and I'm not leaving until I have it."

"*Yours?* You've been gone two months, Ronan. What makes you think anything is still *yours?*"

Tossing the roses to the ground, Ronan set his hands on either side of the door and leaned in. "Laura, I've been on a bloody plane for ten hours, listening to a teenage girl list the reasons she is to be adored. I've had her mother bitching about everything from the type of bottled water on the jet to the fluffiness of her pillow. I'm a man on the edge, love. All I've thought of for these last weeks is getting back to my house on the cliffs and seeing my damned *dog*. I'm not leaving without him."

The door was yanked open suddenly and there she stood. Five feet nine inches of curvy blonde with a pair of blue eyes as clear and lovely as a summer sky. Even in her worn jeans and button-down white shirt, she took his damned breath away, and he resented that fact down to his bones.

She kept one hand on the door and the other braced against the doorjamb as if she'd be enough to keep him out if he decided he wanted in.

Ronan glanced down and saw *his* dog leaning into her with slavish adoration. He scowled at the animal he called Beast, and the dog paid him no attention whatsoever. "A few weeks gone and you've dismissed me?" he asked the dog in a withering tone. "What kind of loyalty is that from man's best friend?"

The dog whined and leaned even more heavily into Laura's side until she staggered a little under his weight.

"A 'best friend' wouldn't have abandoned him," Laura said.

"He wasn't put out into a jungle forced to hunt for his own food," Ronan countered. "My cousin Sean—"

"Left him with me when he went back to Ireland. You can see now that Beast is fine. He's happy here. With me."

"That may be," Ronan told her after sparing his traitorous hound another hard glare. "But he's not yours, is he?"

"He's in my house. That makes him mine."

"He's only *in* your house because Sean asked you to look out for him until I got back."

And for that, Ronan owed his cousin a punch in the face. Called back to Ireland unexpectedly, Sean had asked Laura to watch Beast in order to save the animal a monthlong stay in a kennel. Which Ronan hadn't found out about until it was too late to change anything. Yes, it had been the right choice for the dog. But for Ronan?

He hadn't seen Laura since he ended their affair two months ago. Though he couldn't exactly claim to have shut her out of his mind. Hell, he had taken the bodyguard job for the teenage singer himself, rather than handing it to one of his employees, only so that he could get a little distance from the woman standing so temptingly close to him at the moment. Distance hadn't helped. He'd thought of her. Dreamed of her, and awakened nearly every morning with his body tight and ready for her.

Even now, the lush, slightly floral scent of her reached out to him as if to tease every sense memory he had of touching her, tasting her, being inside her...

"Ronan," she said in a patient tone that interrupted his musings, "we both know Beast is better off with me. You're not exactly a good dog parent—"

"I'm not his father, I'm his bloody owner," Ronan countered.

She ignored him. "Soon enough you'll be going back to Ireland and—"

"Taking Beast with me," he finished for her.

In truth, he hadn't really considered what he would do with Beast when his time in America was over. But right now, the decision seemed an easy one. Even fighting the quarantine laws to get the dog home to Ireland would seem like a vacation after dealing with Laura Page.

Jaw tight, he looked deeply into those calm blue eyes and wondered if she was as unaffected by him as she seemed. Had she forgotten him so quickly? Gotten over him so completely? A lowering thought for a man to consider.

Brushing aside what had once been between them, he said, "Beast is mine, and I always intended to take him home to Ireland with me when I go. Nothing's changed."

"Sure it has," she said, taking a step toward him, dislodging the dog so that he nearly toppled over. "You have a dog back home, right?"

"Aye. Deirdre."

"And it's been how long since you've seen her?"

"That's nothing to do with this."

"It's *everything* to do with it," she countered, folding her arms beneath her breasts. "A dog needs more than a visit every couple of months. A dog needs love. Companionship. Someone he can count on. Someone who will *be* there."

Frowning, Ronan looked hard at her. This was the reason he had stepped back from their relationship in the first place. The woman had hearth and home and forever practically stenciled on her forehead. She was a woman who wanted and *deserved* to be loved. He just wasn't the man to give that to her. So he'd ended their affair before things got even more complicated than they had been already.

"Are you talking about Beast now, Laura, or yourself?"

She gaped at him. "Your ego knows no bounds, does it? Do you really think I've been sitting here moping? Missing you?"

Actually, yes. He did. And the more fired up she got, the more he knew she was no more over him than he was her.

"This isn't about us, Ronan. It's about Beast, and you can't have him. You don't *deserve* him."

Before he could counter, she slammed the door in his face and Ronan heard the lock snap into place. Stunned, he stared at the closed door for a long minute. He could hardly believe it. No one shut a door in Ronan Connolly's face, for pity's sake.

He heard her inside, cooing to Beast, assuring him that he was safe from bullies and that was nearly enough to have Ronan pounding on her door again. But he thought better of it. Let her believe she'd won this battle. It would make her complacent and that much easier to get around later.

Still furious, he turned sharply, stomped on the fallen roses and left.

But he'd be back. Connollys didn't know how to quit.

"It's all right, sweetie," Laura said to Beast as she scrubbed the top of his head and scratched behind his ears. "The mean man is gone."

Laura was trembling by the time she heard Ronan's sports car fire up and zoom off. Oh, not from the argument. She had known that confrontation was coming for weeks. But actually seeing him again had been much harder than she'd thought it would be.

Looking up into those dark blue eyes of his, she'd watched them flash with temper and had been just as stirred as when she'd seen them darken with passion or glitter with a cool, businesslike gleam.

Tall, broad-shouldered, with chestnut hair that showed just a hint of red in the sunlight, he wore business suits and jeans with the same casual air that made him both intimidating and irresistible. And apparently two months apart hadn't dimmed her reaction to him at all.

From the moment he had first walked into her real estate office several months ago, Laura had known that she was in trouble. Oh, she and her sister had sold homes to unspeakably rich people before, but there had never been the slightest temptation to fit herself into their world. With Ronan, it had been different from the start.

Everything in her still wanted him, even though her mind knew better. He'd been out of her life for two months and that was as it should be. After all, she had known going into that mind-dazzling affair that it couldn't last. He was rich; she wasn't. He was Ferrari and she was Volkswagen. He lived in Ireland. And she'd be staying in California.

She sighed a little, then looked down at the dog each of them wanted. Beast was big, at least a hundred pounds and his black hair was full and shaggy, clumps of it usually falling across his eyes. No one knew what mixture of breeds he might be, but privately, Laura had often thought a pony must have been involved somewhere in his lineage.

Now, Beast looked up at her as if sympathizing with the situation, and Laura smiled.

"Sure," she whispered, still stroking Beast's head, "I knew Ronan would be trouble from the first. But a gorgeous, successful man with an Irish accent that makes my bones melt? How was I supposed to fight that?"

The dog gave her one long swiping kiss and she laughed. In his own way, Beast was as charming as his master—just another reason she wouldn't give him up. Then she stood and walked to the kitchen, hearing Beast's claws clatter on the floorboards behind her.

"Well," her sister, Georgia, spoke up from the kitchen table. "That was dignified."

Laura poured herself a cup of coffee, then carried it across the room to take the chair opposite her sister. "I wasn't going for dignified."

"Luckily."

She already knew Georgia's opinion on the whole situation with Ronan—namely, *Never mix business with pleasure*—and she really didn't want to go into it all again. Laura avoided her sister's all-too-perceptive stare by sliding her own gaze around the comfortable kitchen. The soft yellow walls combated the gray day outside. White appliances gleamed and the black granite countertops shone like obsidian. The chrome-and-glass table sat before a bay window that overlooked the backyard where the few trees stood nearly bare in the autumn weather.

Georgia tapped her finger against the glass tabletop until Laura finally looked at her.

"Georgia, I'm not going to talk about this."

"Fine," her sister said, setting her computer tablet down and flipping the lid over the screen. "I'll talk. You listen. Did you really think Ronan wasn't going to show up demanding his dog back?"

"Of course not." Beneath the table, Beast dropped to the floor, laying his heavy body across the tops of her feet. His heavy, solid warmth was a balm. "I knew he would come."

And a part of her had been anticipating seeing him again. Even though she knew it was useless. That they didn't have a future together. That he had ended their amazingly hot affair before they could get too involved. None of that seemed to matter. He had been pretty much completely on her mind from the moment she had met him.

"And your solution to this problem is to hold his dog hostage?"

"Not his dog anymore. Sean brought him to me, remember?"

"Yes. To hold for Ronan until he got back." Georgia picked up her coffee and leaned back in her chair.

Georgia's blond hair was a more subtle shade than Laura's and cut into a short swing that ended at her jawline. Her eyes were a darker blue, her body curvier and her heart a little more hardened. But she was loyal to the bone and Laura's best friend as well as her sister.

"What's this really about, Laura? Are you trying to get back at Ronan?" She cradled her cup between her hands. "Teach him a lesson? Hurt him like he did you when he broke up with you?"

"I wouldn't do that," she said, a little stung that Georgia would think she could. "Besides, he didn't hurt me. I always knew that affair would end."

"Sure, but it's better to be the end*er* not the end*ee*."

In spite of everything Laura laughed a little. "Those are not even words."

"They should be," Georgia said with a quick grin. "Anyway, I'm just saying, this is not only about the Beast and you know it. The least you could do is admit it."

Why should she? Laura frowned, opened her laptop and pushed the power button. The fan whirred and lights flashed as the computer hummed to life. And while she waited, she thought about what Georgia had said. Maybe it did sting to know that Ronan could end their affair so easily and then just walk away without a backward glance. Maybe it had hurt to know that he hadn't felt what she had. Maybe she still experienced a twinge of pain at all she had lost in the last couple of months.

But she had her home. Her sister. And now, a dog. What more could she ask for, really? If a little voice inside whispered *How about love?* She ignored it. Laura had tried love, and it hadn't worked out. Then she'd tried a hot and sexy, no-strings-attached affair with Ronan and that hadn't worked, either.

"Maybe it's time to consider a convent," she mused.

"Yeah," Georgia said on a short laugh. "Because you do so well with authority."

Frowning at her sister, Laura was forced to concede that Georgia had a point. After all, if she did well taking orders, she would still be working for Manny Toledo's real estate office instead of trying to build an empire of her own with Georgia.

Beast snored from under the table and Laura smiled even as a trickle of guilt rippled through her before she deliberately squashed it. Ronan just didn't want to admit that she was right, that Beast would be better off with her.

"This is all his fault," she murmured. "Yes, he owns Beast. But that's not enough. A dog needs someone to love. To count on. Ronan can't go flying off around the world and expect everything to be right there waiting for him when he gets back."

"Uh-huh. And we both know you're not really talking about the dog."

She frowned at her sister. The more she thought about it, the more certain she became that she was doing the right thing. Beast needed more than Ronan could provide and besides, the dog had become a part of her life. She loved him, and she wasn't going to give him up.

As she'd had to give up too much already.

For a moment or two, her heart ached and the sting of tears filled her eyes. But she blinked them back and lifted her chin. It was done, and maybe some dreams shouldn't come into reality anyway. Besides, she had a home she loved, her sister to share it with and a business that she and Georgia were working hard to grow.

Speaking of...

"Can we just talk about work?" Laura deliberately avoided looking at Georgia, by staring instead at the laptop screen going through its wake-up routine.

"Okay then, we'll do a little more avoidance therapy."

"Appreciate it." Laura was grateful for the reprieve.

"So," Georgia said. "Our beloved landlord is jacking the rent up in six months—"

"What?"

"But, he's also offered to lower the price if we still want to buy the building."

"Hike the rent and lower his selling price? How does that make sense?"

"It doesn't," Georgia agreed. "But as long as he's in charge, he can pretty much do what he wants. And our lease is up in six months, so…"

It felt good to get her mind off of Ronan, if only for a few minutes. Together, she and Georgia owned A Brand New Page real estate office and rented a small building on Pacific Coast Highway in Newport Beach. The rent was astonishing, but that area of Orange County was renowned for high rents. To sell the kinds of homes Laura and Georgia specialized in, they had to be in the center of it all.

"Why's he willing to lower the price on the building?"

"Got me," Georgia admitted with a shrug. "But the market's down and he knows it. Plus, his wife wants to move to Montana to be closer to their grandchildren."

Their own parents had up and moved to the wilds of Oregon five years ago, Laura remembered and wistfully almost envied them the courage it took to pack up and go. To discover new places, see new things. But she was rooted in California and couldn't see herself living anywhere else.

"So all we need is a giant down payment."

"Yes," Georgia agreed wryly. "That's all."

"Okay, won't be easy, but if we really work the next few months, we should be able to swing it. I could take out a second on this place and—"

"No." Georgia spoke up fast and firm. "That's crazy, Laura. You're not going to risk your home for this."

"Our home," she corrected.

"Thanks for that, but I still say no. We'll find another way."

Thankfully, even in a bad housing market, there were always a handful of people looking for upscale homes. Enough of those commissions and they'd be able to manage it.

"Okay then, we'll find a way to make it work."

"Now see," Georgia said, catching her sister's eye, "why is it you can be positive about our prospects for getting enough money together to buy the building but not about Ronan?"

"Can we not?" She stared down at her laptop, *willing* the darn thing to boot up already. Why did it take so long? She could be typing, entering information, focusing on work and more able to shut out Georgia's questions.

"I'm supposed to be the cynical one," her sister pointed out. "I am the one with the loser ex-husband. The one who had to move in with you when she got divorced because said loser took everything out of our bank accounts on his way out of town with Busty the Cheerleader."

Laura laughed shortly at the description. It was dead-on. Georgia's ex-husband had been a football coach at a small college in Ohio. Two years ago, when their season ended, the beloved coach and the head cheerleader—who also happened to be the Page sisters' distant cousin—ran off to Hawaii, taking every cent out of a joint account and most of Georgia's self-confidence.

It had taken her sister a while to work her way

through the betrayal and the humiliation of being tossed aside. But finally, the Page family temper had come in handy and Georgia had finally gotten angry. Much easier to live with than feeling sad—as Laura knew all too well.

"So," Georgia said, "I know why I don't trust men in the slightest. But my question is, are you ragging on Ronan because of what Thomas did to you?"

Thomas Banks. Her ex-fiancé. Five years ago, she had lost a dream, but it was so long ago now, that she barely remembered why she had thought herself in love with the man anyway.

"No. This is different. Thomas was supposed to be forever—well, until he broke up with me in favor of Dana—"

"May she'll go blind from the sun glinting off that tacky huge ring he bought her," Georgia put in.

"Good image, thanks!" Laura took a deep breath. "Anyway, losing Thomas didn't really hurt, Georgia. I don't think I ever loved him and he deserved better."

"So did you," Georgia put in.

Smiling, Laura said, "And I shouldn't let myself be hurt by Ronan, either. I knew going in that he was just temporary. He's danger. I'm cozy. I'm stay at home, he's adventure. Never the twain is going to meet or whatever."

"And yet, you kept his dog."

There was that small ping of guilt again. Especially when she recalled the dumbfounded expression on Ronan's face when she refused to hand the dog over. "Well, it wasn't Beast's fault who his owner was."

"Was?"

Beast whined in his sleep, and Laura reached a hand

down to pat him. "Beast is mine now, and he's going to stay mine."

"Good luck with that."

She'd need it. Yes, Ronan had left, but he'd be back. Laura knew that. Ronan Connelly didn't accept defeat. Ever. Ronan was the kind of man who *made* things happen to suit himself. He had built his company into the premier private security business in the world. He traveled by private jet. Knew the famous and the infamous and swept through life with the confidence of a gladiator.

Which was both attractive and annoying. Impossible to have a good argument with a man who never thought he was wrong.

"This isn't really about the dog anyway," Georgia reminded her softly, "and we both know it."

Laura's gaze flicked to her sister's, and she braced herself. She didn't want to talk about this.

But Georgia was too stubborn to let it go.

"You can't blame him for something he didn't even know about."

"I'm not blaming him," Laura countered, though a part of her did, as ridiculous as that sounded. "I'm really not. Ronan's in the past, that's all. That affair of ours had an expiration date stamped on it. I knew that going in."

"Doesn't have to be over," her sister suggested.

"I'm not the one who ended it, remember?"

When Georgia would have argued, Laura spoke up fast. "He's not here forever, Georgia. He's going back to Ireland and we both know it. Well, I live *here*. And besides all of that, we want different things. Move in different worlds. It's just…doomed."

"And you're not going to tell him what's behind all of this? Don't you think he's got a right to know?"

"Maybe he does." Laura shifted her gaze to the trees outside and watched the last few yellowing leaves flutter in the wind before snapping free of the branches and flying off in a twisting dance. Rain pelted from the sky in a burst and tapped at the windowpanes like impatient fingertips against a table.

Funny, their mother had always hated fall and winter. She'd actually called autumn the Death of Hope season because it would be so long until summer again. Funny that she'd chosen to move to such a rainy place. Laura hadn't thought of that in years. Now, it seemed unerringly apt.

Because in this Death of Hope season, she was finally accepting that what she had had with Ronan was over. Finished. Hope was ridiculous when there was absolutely no reason for it.

Turning her gaze back to her sister's, Laura said, "What point is there in telling him that I miscarried his baby?"

"You said it yourself," her sister pointed out gently. "It was *his* baby. Maybe that's point enough."

But it wouldn't change anything, Laura thought. And what if she told him and he didn't care? She didn't think she wanted to find out what Ronan's reaction would have been to almost being a father.

Two

He didn't go home.

Instead, Ronan went to work.

Even with jetlag clawing at him, he knew he was in no mood to rest. At their new office in Newport Beach, his company, Cosain—Irish Gaelic for 'defend'—was just taking root. Situated on Pacific Coast Highway, the two-story building was small, but elegant, with a view of the sea. More important, Cosain was now in the center of one of the wealthiest communities per capita in the United States.

Here, the powerful and the paranoid lived, exactly the kind of clientele Cosain depended on. Here, Ronan was building the American branch of his company.

Of course, there were other security companies out there. Some very good ones. Like King Security. Also headquartered in California, though they'd opened up a European branch in Cadria several months ago.

Ronan smiled to himself. If the Kings moved into his territory, it was only right that he move into theirs. Besides, Cosain didn't go after the same jobs as the Kings. They specialized in security for buildings, events. Cosain specialized in personal security. Bodyguards. And if it pissed off the King family to have Ronan's company here, then that he considered a bonus. Not that the King cousins weren't good guys. They were. But competition was healthy, wasn't it? Business rivalries always inspired everyone to be their best. And Ronan being in what the Kings would no doubt consider their territory just made his success that much sweeter.

Ronan wasn't a man easily satisfied, even with success. There was always more to be found. And in this community of celebrity and money, Ronan was going to make Cosain the most talked about game in town.

Winning. It was about winning. Ronan had learned that early from his father. A ruthless man, the elder Connolly had made a fortune by buying up badly run businesses and turning them around. He used to say the first thing to do was separate the wheat from the chaff—firing the dead weight and promoting the ones as ambitious as himself. He hadn't made many friends along the way, but he had taught his son that winning—coming out on top—was everything.

Ronan walked through the ground floor, his heels sounding out against the gleaming hardwood. His sharp-eyed glance took everything in. Pale green walls were dotted with paintings by local artists and by framed photos of grateful clients. Though most of those he worked for preferred to fly under the radar and not have their personal business known, there were always the celebrities who came alive at the sight of a camera.

There were a few comfortable couches, a low-slung

table with an array of magazines fanned out on top of it. A pedestal table held a crystal vase filled with bright blossoms that scented the air like springtime.

A tidy receptionist sat at a desk and she nodded warily at him as he strode past. "Morning, Mr. Connolly."

He nodded and went past her, disregarding her nervousness. Ronan's mind was already busy with racing thoughts—not all of them about his business.

He took the short flight of stairs to the landing and then to the second floor above. The bustle of this floor, associates at their computers, muted phone conversations and the purr of a printer, soothed him. Centered him. This was why he'd come to California. This was what was important in his life. Not a woman. Not a dog.

Business.

What the Connollys did best.

He'd had it hammered into him from a young age that a man took hold of his life and shook it until it fell into place. Well, he'd done just that, though he knew that if his father were still alive, the old tyrant would refuse to be impressed.

Didn't matter. What he did, he did for himself, not to please a long dead parent who had never approved of him anyway. He made a sharp left and headed for his own office.

"Mr. Connolly!"

He recognized Brian Doherty's voice, but didn't slow down. Brian had come with him from Ireland to help get the new branch up and running. He'd been with Ronan long enough to know his boss slowed down for no one.

"What is it?" he asked, even as he reached for the sheaf of papers Brian held out to him.

"The Bensons. They'll be here in a few minutes for the meeting you scheduled from the plane."

"Right." Shaking his head in disgust, Ronan realized he'd actually *forgotten* about the meeting with all the drama at Laura's house. The woman was not only affecting his life but his business. Just went to show how tired he actually was.

Turning his mind to the task at hand, he pushed thoughts of Laura aside to be dealt with later and mentally reviewed the Benson file. Benson Electronics. Jeremy and Maria, wealthy, devoted parents of two teenagers who had already burned through a series of bodyguards from lesser companies. Now they wanted to hire two of Cosain's guards on a long-term contract. Just the kind of client Ronan preferred.

"Send them in as soon as they arrive," he said, stepping into his office. He closed the door, and stalked across the room. Taking a quick look around, Ronan assured himself that nothing had changed in his absence. Six weeks was a long time. If he hadn't had Brian onsite and access to Skype, satellite phones and fax machines, he never would have been able to take a job himself at this stage. But Cosain was a well-oiled machine, and though they were new to this country, Ronan had brought along much of his already trained staff to ensure a smooth transition.

Frowning, Ronan sat down at his desk, then reached for the phone and stabbed in a number. In a moment or two, the connection was made and on the second ring a familiar voice spoke up, the music of Ireland coloring his words.

"Ronan. That you?"

"Who else would it be calling from my phone?" he countered.

"Thought it would be one of your minions as I knew you were out protecting that awful child singer."

"I'm back," he said, though he had to admit the child in question really was terrible. How she became a sensation was beyond Ronan. "And I've been to Laura's to collect my dog."

"Ah, Beast," Sean said. "And how is he then?"

"I wouldn't know. Barely caught a glimpse of him." And that fact was still irritating. No one got the best of Ronan Connolly. Yet, for the moment, Laura seemed to have managed the impossible.

"Well why the hell didn't you?"

"She wouldn't let me in her bloody house," Ronan ground out.

"Ah. Still angry then, is she?"

"Angry she is, about what I've no idea."

Sean actually chuckled. "She seemed no fan of you when I spoke with her last."

"It makes no sense," he muttered, more to himself than his cousin. The woman had been cool as cream when he'd ended their relationship two months ago. She'd not argued with him over it. Though he thought back now and remembered the flash in her eyes as she stood in her doorway blocking his entrance like a virgin guarding her virtue.

"Women are confusing creatures at the best of times," Sean said. "Maybe she's simply wanting you back again, though why she would is beyond my imaginings."

Ronan scraped one hand across his face. Was that what this was all about? Did she want him back in her bed and thought holding his dog a prisoner a way to accomplish it? "If that's all it is, why doesn't she just bloody say so?"

"If I understood women," Sean told him, "I'd write

a book and make a fortune selling it to the rest of the men in the world."

Good point, Ronan thought.

"So, how will you get Beast back if she won't let you in the house?"

"I'm working on that. But why the devil you took *my* dog to my *ex* is still beyond me. What were you thinking, Sean?"

"I had to move fast. The Knock airport was meeting on whether or not to allow my jets a slot in their schedule. Had to be here to win the battle."

That he could understand, Ronan thought grimly. Business came first in the Connolly family. And his cousin was no different than he. Sean had been working for months, trying to wedge his airline, Irish Air, into the flight schedule at Knock, an international airport in the west of Ireland. "And did you win?"

"Of course," Sean said. "Irish Air will now be flying to the Continent three flights a day. To start," he added. "We'll build from there."

"Congratulations then. I might not push my fist into your face after all."

"It's appreciated," Sean said with a laugh. "Though I remember the last time we brawled, it was your nose that was broken, not mine."

"True." Ronan lifted one hand and rubbed a fingertip over the bump in his nose. "I still owe you for that."

"No hurry to pay me back on that one." The roar of a jet taking off sounded in the background and Sean waited until it died away before continuing. "How much longer will you be in California then?"

"Not sure," Ronan admitted, swinging his desk chair around to stare out at the sweep of sea and sky. Dark gray clouds roiled overhead while the ocean, the color of pewter, frothed with whitecaps. The view reminded him of home—dark skies, wind howling, the churning ocean—and he suddenly missed Ireland with a sharp pang. "I've yet to find a place suitable for the permanent offices. Until I do that, I'll be staying."

"So there's time then to win your dog back from Laura."

Scowling at the phone, Ronan snapped, "There's no reason to 'win' him back. He's mine, isn't he?"

"Well then, go claim your mutt and let me get back to the meeting you've pulled me out of."

Ronan hung up soon after and was still frowning when there was a sharp knock on his door. Pushing thoughts of Laura, Sean and anything else that wasn't centered on business from his mind, Ronan stood and called, "Come in."

Brian opened the door, then stepped back to allow a couple to enter the room. "Mr. and Mrs. Benson, Ronan Connolly."

"Thank you, Brian," Ronan said, and waved a hand at the chairs in front of his desk. Speaking to the husband and wife, he said, "Please, sit down."

"Thank you for seeing us," Maria said, folding her hands over the top of the designer bag she held in her lap.

Ronan nodded and shifted his gaze to her husband. "Happy to. What can Cosain do to help?"

As Jeremy Benson started talking, Ronan lasered his focus on the task at hand. Just as later he would use that same focus on the problem of Laura.

Beast was snoring.

It was a comforting sound, since Laura was pleased at least one of them was getting some sleep.

Outside, the storm was still raging, sending fits of wind-driven rain pelting at her windows. It was a cozy sound, one she normally would have enjoyed. Tonight, it was simply background noise to the thoughts churning in her brain.

She kept hearing Ronan's voice in her mind, the music of his accent and the way it deepened and thickened when he was angry. She saw his mouth, tight and grim, his eyes flashing and couldn't help remembering the sizzle in the air between them.

Trying to sleep was pointless, since she couldn't seem to settle, so instead, she sat propped up in bed, a romance novel open in her hands, lamplight spilling across a page she had already read ten times. It was infuriating to admit that Ronan could so shatter her thoughts she couldn't even concentrate on reading.

When she heard the front door open and softly close, she assumed it was Georgia coming back early from her date. Not a good sign, Laura thought and wished her sister could find happiness again. She thought about getting up and checking on her sister, but then they would be drawn into conversation about Georgia's failed date and Laura's failed romance. No, thank you.

Turning slightly, she reached out one hand to the pillow beside her and remembered Ronan lying there, giving her that slow, sly smile that never failed to turn her insides into swirls of lava. She stroked her fingertips over the cold sheets and pretended that she felt instead a warm, muscled Irishman.

"It was good," she whispered to the empty room. "For a while anyway, it was very good."

Her bedroom door opened, and she turned to face her sister.

Ronan's gaze locked with hers. Then he saw her hand, stretched out across the mattress. "Miss me?"

She jolted up in bed, her book sailing to the floor to land with a thump.

His hair was damp. Raindrops on his black knit sweater glittered like diamonds in the lamplight and his eyes were fixed on her. Her heart rate jumped into high gear even as a burn of something familiar began inside her.

"What the— How did you— Why are you—"

"I've still got the key you gave me," Ronan said, holding it up for her to see before tucking it into the pocket of his faded jeans.

"Well, give it back."

"I'll not be doing that," he said, moving into the room and closing the door behind him.

Laura hitched backward on the bed, plastering herself against the headboard and drawing her pale lemon duvet practically up to her chin. A little late to be protecting herself around Ronan. But knowing her own body's reactions to him, better safe than sorry.

That deep burning sensation spread like a wildfire, lighting up her bloodstream and sending her hormones into overdrive. What kind of penance was she paying that even furious with him, even knowing she had to let him go from her life, she still wanted him so badly her whole body ached with it?

"What're you doing here, Ronan?" she demanded, curling her fingers into the silky duvet material as if she were holding on to a lifeline.

"Came to talk, Laura," he said, strolling closer to the bed. Closer to *her*.

"There's nothing to talk about, and by the way, why do you still have my key?" And how had she forgotten to get it back? Well, to be fair, when he gave her the speech on how it wasn't working out and that they wouldn't be seeing each other again, she'd felt too bruised to remember to ask for it back.

Which she was kicking herself for now.

He patted the pocket where he'd deposited the key. "You gave it to me."

"We were together at the time," she pointed out and winced as her own voice went a little high. Beneath their conversation, Beast's snoring continued on.

"Could be again," he said, then glanced down at Beast so he didn't see Laura's eyes go wide.

"Easy to see why you want to keep the Beast," he noted wryly. "A vicious guard dog such as this one would make you feel safe."

Beast snored even louder.

"He's company."

"Aye," Ronan mused, "quite the conversationalist." He bent down, rubbed one hand across Beast's exposed stomach and said, "Wake up, you lazy hound."

The dog's eyes reluctantly opened. He saw Ronan and rolled over, pushing himself up high enough to welcome his former owner with a kiss.

Ronan laughed and the sound seemed to rumble through the room before settling in the pit of Laura's stomach and jittering there. She tried to remind herself that they were exes. Tried to remember how she'd felt the night he left her. Tried to remember the pain she'd suffered later when she lost—

Steeling herself, she said, "Ronan, you don't belong here. You should leave."

"But I *am* here, and I'm not ready to go just yet."

In the lamplight, his blue eyes shone and she read

amusement in their depths, which only served to make her angrier. A good thing.

"Yes, you're here. Without invitation."

"And would you have invited me in?"

"No."

"There you are then." He shrugged and took a seat at the end of the bed. Beast moved to lay his big head on Ronan's thigh and both man and dog watched her.

He was far too close.

"So, your guard dog doesn't seem to mind me being here."

Feeling oddly compelled to defend the dog, she said, "He knows I'm not in danger from you."

Ronan tilted his head to one side as his gaze speared into hers. "I wouldn't be so sure of that, were I you."

Her stomach did a slow swirl and spin. She shoved one hand through her hair, then grabbed up the duvet again and held it even closer. "Ronan, you should go."

"No. Not until you tell me what it is that's really at the heart of all of this."

"I don't know what you're talking about." She scooted even farther from him, smacking her back against the headboard.

"Aye, you do, but for some reason, you're not telling me." Nodding, he glanced down at the dog, then back to her. "It's not about Beast at all, is it? There's something that's driving you."

"If there is, it's none of your business," she countered.

Outside, the wind moaned under the eaves and the rain hammered at the window glass. He was watching her as if waiting for her to speak up and give him exactly what he wanted. Which was just so like him. Well, Laura wasn't going to satisfy his curiosity.

"You broke up with me, remember? How did you

put it? Oh, yes." As if she could forget. "I believe your exact words were, *It's been a grand time for the both of us and now it's done.*"

He frowned thoughtfully. "And you weren't ready for it, were you, Laura love?"

She gritted her teeth at the easy endearment, knowing it meant nothing.

Smiling now, he gave Beast one last pat on the head, then stood up and paced off a few steps before turning and walking back to her. He stopped in the circle of the lamplight and looked down at her thoughtfully. "You see, I've done some thinking, and I've figured out what the problem is."

"Congratulations," she snapped, scooting to the other side of the mattress. She couldn't stay in her bed and talk to him. It was disconcerting. Tempting. And oh, how she hated to admit that, even to herself. Once her feet were firmly on the floor she added, "Now, go away."

Still smiling, he walked around the bed and came close to her. Here, there were more shadows. The golden glow of the lamp didn't reach this far. She refused to back up and let him corner her against the wall. So she stood her ground.

"Don't you want to know what it is I've discovered?"

"Will it make you leave if I say yes?"

He grinned. "It might."

"Fine." She crossed her arms over her chest. "What is it then?"

"This isn't about keeping my dog from me," he said, reaching out to lay both hands on her bare shoulders.

God, why had she worn a tank top to sleep in? She should have worn flannel. Head to toe.

Heat from his palms slid into her system and washed through her like a fever. She had to fight her own reaction to him. Her own instinct to lean into that broad chest. To go up and kiss that mouth that had done so many amazing things to her such a short while ago.

"I know what you really want, Laura," he said and bent down until they were eye to eye. "And I came here tonight to tell you, you don't have to try this hard to get back into my bed. You've only to ask."

Time stopped.

Later, Laura would think she must have been struck dumb to be able to remain speechless for so much as a second after that incredible statement. But she wasn't quiet for long.

"You dolt."

"What?"

She brushed his hands off her arms, and then planted both palms on his chest and shoved hard enough to rock him back a couple of steps.

"Neanderthal."

"There's no reason for all of this, Laura," he said, that accent of his dancing along her nerve endings, promising romance.

She fought past it.

"Are you crazy? You really think I took Beast to get *you* back?"

"What other reason would there be?" he asked, irritation now sparking in eyes that were still glinting with desire.

"Oh, I don't know. Because I felt sorry for the dog? Because I didn't want to see him abandoned? Because I think you're a big jerk who doesn't deserve Beast?"

"Now just hang on—"

"No."

"So you're saying you feel nothing for me," he said,

taking a stand, unmovable no matter how hard she pushed.

"I am," she said, glaring at him since that was all that was left to do.

"You're a liar."

"You—"

He swooped in then. Simply grabbed her up, yanked her in close and claimed her mouth in a kiss that stole what breath she had and fogged her mind. Sensations coursed through her in a wild stream. The feel of his mouth on hers. The taste of him. His strong arms holding her pinned to his chest. All of these things and more tied her up into so many knots, Laura was helpless to unravel any of them.

And she didn't care to.

Instead, she surrendered to the lush moment. Gave herself up to the rush of being in Ronan's arms again. Even though she knew it was a mistake she would regret deeply in the morning, for this one instant, she simply let herself feel.

And just as she was really beginning to enjoy herself, it was over.

He let her go and took a step back. Even with her mind reeling, she saw amusement in his eyes again and wanted to kick herself.

"I think we've both got our answers now," he said.

"Get out," she whispered.

Behind them, Beast whimpered.

"All right."

Surprised, she watched him warily. "Just like that?"

He shrugged. "I'll not stay when you tell me to go. But I won't *stay* away, Laura. What's between you and me isn't done, is it?"

"Yes," she said, realizing how stupid that sounded

coming from a woman who had just willingly given herself up to a kiss hot enough to burn down the house. "It is."

He reached out, cupped her cheek in one palm and stroked her skin with his thumb. "We'll see about that, won't we?"

"Why, Ronan? You left two months ago without looking back. Why do you care now?"

He let his hand drop. "There's something you're not telling me, Laura. You want me, that's easy enough to see…"

She grimaced and huffed out a breath.

"But it's more than that, and I think you know it. There's something…else. And I'll know what it is before we're done."

She was in trouble, and she knew it. Her own body betrayed her when she was around Ronan. And she knew, if he put his mind to it, he would discover the truth about the surprise pregnancy that had ended in a miscarriage. Maybe Georgia was right. Maybe she should just tell him.

But the baby was *her* secret. *Her* loss.

She'd known from the first that there was no future in a relationship with Ronan. The day he'd walked into their real estate office and told her in brief, concise terms exactly what he wanted. What he needed from her. And maybe it had been the Irish accent that had done most of the seducing. But it hadn't mattered in the end. She'd allowed herself to be swept up into an affair that had burned so brightly, it had gone to ash before its time.

"Now, see there," he whispered. "It's that flash of something…off…in your eyes that intrigues me. You've a secret, Laura."

"No, I don't," she lied.

He laughed and shook his head. "All women have their secrets, darlin'," he said, "and all men find a way to reveal them."

"Sure of yourself, aren't you?" Of course he was. It was one of the things she'd liked most about him. At first.

"Be foolish of me not to be, wouldn't it?"

He would see it like that. Laura had never known a man as self-confident, as completely convinced of the rightness of everything he did, as Ronan Connolly. She envied that as much as it irritated her. Which was, she was forced to admit, quite a lot.

He turned to go.

"What about Beast?" she asked.

He shot a look at the dog that had moved to stand in front of Laura, like a big, furry shield. A smile curved Ronan's mouth briefly. "He can stay with you. For now."

Laura's fingers curled into the dog's long, shaggy hair. "Ronan?"

He stopped and looked back at her. The lamplight didn't climb as high as his face, so his features, his eyes, were in shadow when she asked, "Why is it so important to you? Why do you care what my secrets are?"

A long moment of silence stretched out until all she heard was Beast's gentle breathing and the tap of rain at the window. Just as she decided he wasn't going to answer her at all, he spoke.

"Because I want what's mine, Laura Page."

"But I'm not yours."

"You were," he reminded her, "and if those secrets still belong to me, I'll have them before we're done."

He left her then, quietly closing the door behind him. Laura dropped onto the edge of the bed, finally giving in to the weakness in her knees. She lifted one hand to her mouth and swore she could still feel the buzz of his kiss sliding through her.

Then she sighed.

He hadn't returned her key.

Three

Laura got a late start the next morning.

While Georgia was out dealing with business at the post office, Laura stayed home to wait for the locksmith. Once all of the locks had been changed, she felt safe enough to leave Beast at home and go into the office.

Of course, her eyes were gritty from lack of sleep and her temper was more than a little on edge. And it was all Ronan's fault.

This wasn't right, she told herself as she unlocked the real estate office and flipped the sign on the door to 'open'. She was supposed to be free of Ronan. Getting on with her life. Getting him out of her system.

The phone rang and she snatched at it gratefully. "Brand New Page Realty," she said, plastering a smile she didn't feel onto her face.

"You're late today," Ronan answered.

"Had to wait for a locksmith," she told him, with

just a bit of satisfaction. "Oh, feel free to throw that key away now."

He chuckled. "Think I'll be keeping it in the way of a souvenir."

"You want keepsakes now?" she asked, sitting at her desk and riffling through the stack of mail. Bill. Bill. Bill. She sighed, tossed them to the desktop and leaned back in her chair.

Through the front window, the only signs of yesterday's storm were the puddles in the street and the soaked piles of leaves that had been torn from trees. Thanks to the rain, the sky was a brilliant blue and the cold wind that rushed in off the ocean was drying everything out quickly.

"It wasn't so long ago that you were telling me we were through," she reminded him.

"Times change," he countered and as he spoke, a long, black car pulled up in front of her shop.

Laura watched the driver of the car get out and she shook her head as she met Ronan's gaze through the window. He was holding his cell phone to his ear and grinning at her.

"You know, it's illegal to drive in California while holding your phone."

"Ah, but I'm a dangerous man who likes a risk."

He really was dangerous. To her peace of mind if nothing else. But damned if she'd let him know it. She'd spent hours during a long sleepless night berating herself for giving in to that kiss. No way was she going to slip up again.

Ronan was like any other bad habit.

The only way to quit was cold turkey.

"What are you doing here?"

He walked around his car, pushed open the door and

a bell overhead jangled to announce him. Only then did he shut off his phone and tuck it into a pocket of his black slacks. "Giving you another chance to show me how much you want me."

"God, you're an impossibly arrogant man."

"If you think that's insulting, you'd be wrong." He walked farther into the room. "I do wonder though, why you're so on edge around me. Didn't used to be."

"Times change," she shot back, throwing his own words at him as she set the phone back into its cradle.

"I like a woman with a temper," he said. "Call it a flaw."

"The very notion that you're willing to admit to a flaw might ordinarily be a cause for celebration—"

He smiled as if everything she said amused him, and it probably did. That smile of his, along with the accent that seemed to ripple over her skin like a caress was a formidable weapon to a man who already had too many at his disposal.

"You've left Beast at home then?" He glanced around the office then back to her.

"He's fine. And he knows I'll be back."

"Whereas, he wept and pined for me in my absence?" he asked.

Frowning, she shuffled the bills into a neat pile all while keeping one wary eye on him. "Ronan, why are you here?"

"To tell you I'll be gone a few days."

In spite of everything, she felt a ping of disappointment. Stupid. She should be glad he was leaving again. "So you're proving my point about Beast. You're gone more than you're home."

"I would have taken him with me this time," he told her.

"Beast on a plane?"

"Did I mention anything about a plane?"

"No," she had to admit.

"Aren't you going to ask where I'm going?"

"No again," she told him, though she was dying to know. Was he off to protect someone else? Putting himself in danger again? Or just rushing to get away from her again?

"I'll tell you anyway. I'm off to the training grounds where our newest guards are taking their final tests."

He had told her about the bodyguard training all of his employees had to take and pass before coming to work for him. She knew it was out in the desert somewhere, though he had kept the exact location a secret. Security reasons, he had told her, and she remembered being hurt that he didn't trust her enough to be specific.

Seemed he still didn't.

Laura glanced out the window to the busy street beyond, wishing someone—*anyone*—would come inside desperate to find a house. She couldn't count on Georgia showing up, because she was at the post office with a stack of packages to mail and that could take either minutes or hours, depending.

Taking a breath, Laura resigned herself to being alone with Ronan no matter how hard it was. All she had to do was *not* think about that kiss. Better that she remember that he had walked away from her once already.

"So why are you telling me this?" she asked, deliberately keeping a distance from him.

"To give you a chance to miss me, of course."

She blinked at him. "What?"

Ronan smiled easily and leaned against the corner of her desk. Crossing his arms in front of him, he looked her up and down and then met her eyes again. "I want you to think of me while I'm gone."

"Why would I do that?" she demanded, though a part of her knew she would be doing just what he wanted her to. The real question was *why* he wanted her to. "You were gone for six weeks, and I didn't miss you."

"Liar." His eyes flashed knowingly.

"I didn't miss you before, and I won't now, either," she said and hoped she sounded more sure than she felt. "Why would I? You're the one who broke things off between us, Ronan."

"Aye, I did at that, and I'm thinking perhaps that was a mistake…"

"Wow," she muttered, trying to cover the flutter of nerves, "admitting to flaws *and* a mistake all in the same conversation. Maybe you should see a doctor."

He laughed. "What is it, I wonder, about that sharp tongue of yours intrigues me so?"

"I don't want you intrigued, Ronan," she told him and tried to ease past him to head for the file cabinet on the far wall.

She didn't make it. He stopped her with one hand on her arm and the heat of his touch sizzled against her skin.

"Don't you?" he asked, leaning toward her.

"No," she answered, her gaze on his mouth as it came closer and closer— *"No."*

She said it louder this time, and he stopped in response. Narrowing his eyes on her, he cocked his head to one side to study her. "You'd deny us both the kiss we each want?"

"Yes." When he moved in again, she scuttled back. "I meant yes, I would deny us both."

He blew out a breath and straightened up and away

from the desk. His blue eyes were cool, his tone brisk as he said, "Fine then. I'll not push you on this."

"Good."

"For now."

Sunlight streamed through the front window, backlighting Ronan until he looked as if he'd been gilded by angels. Just that thought was enough to make her laugh silently. There was nothing angelic about Ronan Connolly. The man was temptation. He was warm when he chose to be and cold enough to freeze you solid if he thought you were getting too close.

Laura had already lived through that once. She had thought she could be the kind of woman to have a red-hot affair and not think of tomorrow. She'd learned fast—though not fast enough—that she wasn't.

She'd lost her heart to him once. And she'd lost a child. She wasn't prepared to lose more. Those thoughts steeled her spine and had her lifting her chin. "I'm not interested, Ronan."

"Another lie," he said, mouth quirking into a half smile.

"Fine," she snapped, crossing to the file cabinet and blindly yanking open one of the metal drawers. She pulled out a manila folder, not caring which one it was. This was to prove to him she was too busy to play his games. "It's ridiculous to try to pretend that you're not... attractive."

He snorted.

"But," she said pointedly, "I'm not going down that road again. Heck, you're the one who wanted to get *off* the road."

"Will you forever be throwing that back at me?" he wondered aloud.

"Why wouldn't I?" Carrying the folder to her desk,

she scooted past him, then took a stand, figuratively and literally. "We were together three months and you ended it two months ago. Time to move on, don't you think?"

He looked at her again and the flat, steady stare he sent her way had Laura thinking that he was looking into her heart, her mind.

"What I think," he said, "is there's more going on here than you'll say."

"If there is, it's my business," she retorted and dropped the file to her desktop.

"That's where you're wrong." He planted both hands on her desk and leaned in until they were eye to eye. "If you wanted me gone from your life so neatly, Laura Page, you should've returned Beast to me. But you didn't and that tells me you want me bothered. Troubled. And I have to ask myself why.

"So we'll not be finished until I've got my answers." Damn it.

"You can end this today by telling me what it is you're hiding," he told her, lifting one hand to push her hair back behind her ear.

She flinched from his touch, and he frowned. He hadn't liked that, but Laura couldn't let him touch her because every time he did, it weakened her resistance to him.

"Tell me," he whispered, all hint of a smile gone from his face. "Tell me why I see sadness as well as passion in your eyes when you look at me. Tell me why you took Beast and held him hostage. Tell me—"

She shook her head and held up one hand in an effort to stop him. "I don't have to tell you anything, Ronan."

"You don't, but you will."

"Because you say so? I don't think so."

"No," he countered, coming around her desk to stand

beside her. "Because it's eating you up inside to *not* tell me. It's on the tip of your tongue at all times, but you keep biting it back. So let it out, Laura. If you truly want me gone from your life, then tell me."

Well, that was part of the problem, wasn't it? If she told him, she'd have the satisfaction of seeing shock jolt into his eyes, but then he'd be gone, wouldn't he? Really gone, and she didn't know if she was as ready for that as she claimed to be. But it was more than just that. Sharing her secrets would open herself up to the pain of talking about her loss. And she wasn't willing to do that.

The front door opened, the bell jangled a welcome and Georgia stepped inside and stopped dead on the threshold, staring from one to the other of them. "Am I interrupting?"

"Yes," Ronan said.

"No," Laura disagreed.

"Okay, then, it's a draw, and I get to decide," Georgia told them, walking to her desk. "And, since I just spent an hour and a half with the slowest postal employee on the face of the planet, all before coffee, I choose to interrupt."

Ronan's gaze never left Laura's and though she heard her sister speaking, the words were lost and muted, as if coming from a distance. She paid no attention when Georgia left the room and went into the mini-kitchen where the coffee was waiting. She was too tied into knots to do much more than nod at Ronan when he murmured, "I'll be going then."

"Goodbye."

He eased away, walked to the door and gave a quick nod to Georgia before looking back at Laura. "You'll miss me."

Not a question, but she answered anyway.

"No, I won't."

He grinned. "Liar."

Ronan calmed his mind, let his thoughts slide away and paid no attention to the wind rushing in off the desert, stinging his skin with grains of sand. Instead he aimed, setting his sights on the silhouette target a hundred yards away. Slowly, he let out his breath and squeezed the trigger. Then he did it again and again until the clip in his automatic pistol was empty.

Taking off his ear protection, he hooked them around his neck and ejected the empty clip.

"Not bad." Sam Travis walked up beside him, hit a red button on the wall and a humming sound buzzed into the air. The target flew toward them on a wire, the paper fluttering wildly. When it arrived, Sam nodded as he noted twelve shots expertly placed on the silhouette. Six in the head, six in the body, all closely grouped.

"Gotta stay on top," Ronan said, then set his weapon into the zip bag and closed it. It was good to get out on a range and test his own reflexes, his aim. He expected the best of his guards and would accept nothing less from himself.

"You always did push yourself hard."

"No point in doing something if you're not going to be the best, now is there?"

"Suppose not," Sam said, then asked, "So, want to tell me what's weighing on your mind?"

Ronan shot Sam a quick look. Since when was he so easy to read? Hell, all over Ireland, Ronan Connolly was known to have the best poker face in the country. No one could tell what he was thinking. For years, he'd worked at locking down his emotions. Until now he would have said it was second nature.

Irritating to know that his control had slipped enough to allow Sam a glimpse of the turmoil within.

Covering as best he could, he said, "There's nothing."

"Yeah. Sell that to someone who doesn't know you as well as I do."

True, Sam did know him well. The two of them had been friends for five years, since meeting in the Middle East when they were both guarding politicians. That friendship had eventually become a partnership. Ronan had given Sam Travis the start-up capital to open his training facility and now he personally trained all new Cosain employees.

"So, what's got the great Ronan Connolly twisting in the wind?"

Ronan frowned. "Would it do me any good to tell you I don't want to talk about it?"

"What do you think?"

He snorted. "I think you're a pain in the ass."

"That's been said before." Sam leaned back against the hip-high half wall lining the front of the firing range. "Doesn't answer the question though."

No, it didn't. If Sean were here, Ronan might talk things through with his cousin. Then he smiled at the notion. Sean was more determinedly single than even Ronan, so what would the man possibly know about what Ronan was feeling at the moment. Hell, even *he* wasn't sure what his feelings were.

From the long range weapons area, shots echoed in the clear desert air. Here, it was just he and Sam in the waning afternoon light. He took one last stab at keeping his thoughts to himself. "What makes you think there's anything?"

"For one, you don't usually make a surprise visit. For

another, you haven't been on the range in months. So something's bugging you. Anything I can do?"

It had been months since he'd been target shooting. Because he did more desk work than field work these days, it hadn't seemed important. But since getting back from his last job and finding himself at war with Laura Page, Ronan had felt the need to settle himself. So he'd come here. To see his friend. To check on his new recruits. And to lose himself in tasks that required enough focus and concentration that he had none left to spare for the woman currently haunting his thoughts. So far though, even the range hadn't shoved Laura completely from his mind.

It was good to see Sam, whether or not the man was digging too close to what Ronan would rather not talk about. Ronan met his friend's direct gaze and counted himself a lucky man. He wasn't long on family—having only Sean and his widowed mother, Ronan's aunt Ailish—but he had a few *good* friends who more than made up for the lack. Though even the best of friends couldn't help him uncover the mystery that was Laura—or the question as to why the hell he cared.

"I appreciate it, Sam. I do. But—"

"Butt out?"

"Aye," he said with a nod, "to put it bluntly."

Affably, Sam shrugged and smiled. "I can do that—"

"The question is, you see, not what's bugging me," Ronan mused aloud, "it's what's chewing at Laura's insides enough to make *my* life a misery."

"Ah, problem explained."

"How's that?" Ronan asked.

"It's a woman. Therefore, you're screwed."

"That's quite the statement from a happily married man."

"The reason I'm happily married is I don't try to figure Kara out." Sam lifted the collar of his jacket against the desert wind dragging the scent of sand and sage past them. "If she's mad, I apologize."

Ronan could only stare at him. "Apologize for what?"

Sam shrugged. "For whatever she thinks I did."

"And what if you've done nothing?" Ronan thought back and assured himself again that no, he hadn't done a damn thing wrong. All right, perhaps he might have been a bit abrupt in the way he broke things off with her before, but she'd not complained at the time. And hadn't it been her own fault he'd done it at all? Looking at him with those dreamy eyes of hers where plans and futures were so plainly written.

What else could he have done, but pull away so that she got no notions of permanence? He'd made no promises and so hadn't broken any. So what the devil did he have to apologize for?

"We're *male,* Ronan," Sam said on a laugh. "So as far as our women are concerned, we've always done *something.*"

"Well, that's a hell of a thing."

"Is what it is," Sam said with another shrug. "Take it from me. Apologize. Get it over with. It's not as bad as you might think."

Shaking his head, Ronan clapped one hand on his friend's shoulder. "It's sad I am to see what's become of you, Sam. A warrior. Fierce. Afraid of nothing. And now you'll apologize for the sin of being a man."

"Damn straight." Sam grinned. "And flowers wouldn't hurt, either."

"Flowers." Ronan snorted and shook his head. Damned if he'd apologize for doing nothing and hadn't he already tried bringing her flowers? The roses he'd left crushed on her front steps? Remembering had him gritting his teeth. No, he wouldn't be doing that again.

Ronan shifted his gaze to the surrounding desert. Miles and miles of rock and sand and cactus and scraggly Mesquite and not much else. In late fall, the sun was bright and the air was cool, and the continuously blowing wind didn't warm things up any. Ronan was used to cold, given that he was born and raised in Ireland.

But, damn. "You know, I'd give a thousand dollars right now, just to see one bloody tree."

Sam laughed. "The desert's no substitute for Ireland, huh?"

"True enough," he admitted, grateful his friend accepted the change in subject so easily. "I've never seen so much…*brown*."

Ronan hunched deeper into his black leather jacket and shot a mean look at the empty blue sky. "Bloody cold for a desert," he muttered.

Sam laughed again and slapped Ronan's back companionably. "You should be here in the summer. Then we're up in the one-twenties and you're begging for shade."

Shaking his head, he gave his old friend a rueful smile. "Don't know how you stand it out here in the middle of nothing."

His gaze swept his surroundings again as if he still couldn't believe how little was out there. Oh, Sam had given him the speech about how the desert wasn't really empty. There were animals out there, supposedly, cowering behind spindly bushes and thorny cactuses, but Ronan had never seen one.

"I like it," Sam said, staring out at the openness, with its wide stretch of sky and the miles of sand laid out beneath it. "It's quiet."

A barrage of rifle fire impacted that statement and Ronan snorted.

"Usually," Sam amended. "Kara was raised in the desert, in Arizona, so she's happy here. And, when we're not training new guys, we've got thousands of acres to ourselves."

"There is that," Ronan agreed, since he was a man who liked his privacy as well. "But couldn't you plant a bloody tree?"

Shaking his head, Sam said, "I'll get right on it."

"Fine then." Ronan motioned toward the rifle range in the distance. "They're doing well?"

"Yeah, they are. They're a good bunch. Every last one of them's practically a sharpshooter."

Which was why they were in the middle of the bloody desert, Ronan told himself. Hard to train men in long distance firing drills in the middle of the city. Plus, here at the training facility, there were obstacle courses, classrooms and dormitory style lodgings.

The training encompassed everything from hand to hand combat, to short-and long-distance firing exercises and class work on strategies and diplomacy. Each man who came here to be trained as a personal security specialist would, if he passed, be licensed by the state of California and then entrusted with the safety of Cosain's clients.

"All six should graduate, no problem."

Ronan nodded, glad to hear it. The training wasn't cheap, but it was worth every penny. "How's the former marine doing?"

Sam laughed. "Cobb's doing great. Cleared the obstacle course in record time, then scored ten out of ten on the firing range. The man's made for this work."

"Good. I'll have a job for him as soon as he's cleared and licensed."

Ronan continued on, across the rocky ground, in companionable silence with Sam. He had jobs for each of the new trainees once they were ready. For every one man accepted into the training facility, three were rejected out of hand. Those that applied had to be vetted, their backgrounds dissected, their training enhanced.

It didn't matter how well they came recommended or if they were fully competent already. No guard worked for Cosain without going through the company's own instruction. Only the best were hired by Cosain. Ronan expected nothing less than perfection from himself, so he demanded the same from those who worked for him.

In Ronan's opinion, former military made the best bodyguards. They responded well to authority, were at home with weapons and dealing with dangerous situations was nothing new to them.

He knew that most of those who worked for him would never be forced to draw their weapons. The vast majority of guard jobs were rarely more than glorified babysitting gigs and that was fine with Ronan. If his clients felt safer with a Cosain guard around, he was happy to oblige them, even though in his opinion, most people didn't need his services. It was almost as if having a bodyguard was a status symbol. A sign of celebrity. Have a guard and look more important than you actually were.

Of course, there were the other jobs, the occasional situations where lives were at stake. Then, Ronan knew the people he sent out on missions would risk their own lives to save someone else's.

"You miss it?"

Ronan slanted a look at Sam. He knew what the other man was asking. "Not often. You?"

"Nah. Running all over creation's a younger man's game."

"Younger?" Ronan laughed. "Hell, I'm but thirty-four and you just a year older."

"Yeah, and the new recruits out there—" They stopped at the edge of the combat training field and Sam waved one hand at the ten men enduring hand-to-hand instruction. "They're in their twenties, tops."

Ronan looked out over the open space, and considered. Ten years he'd been doing this and for the last three or four of those years, he'd hardly spent any actual time in the field. Hadn't really noticed, but somewhere along the line, he'd become the 'desk guy.' Though something inside him still roared to the surface at the offer of a new job, a new mission, more times than not, he handed that assignment off to one of his men.

Still, his pride told him he was as good as he'd ever been. "We could take 'em," he said.

"I believe you could," Sam agreed, laughing. "But me, I'm an old married man now. Kara doesn't want me out on jobs. And now that she's pregnant, I've got no interest in risking my neck anymore."

"Pregnant?" Stunned, Ronan realized the man looked ecstatic about the possibility of being a father. He would have thought that Sam had no more interest in that than he. And yet here the man was, bursting with pride. A pride, Ronan told himself, he couldn't truly understand. After all, he had never had any interest in being a father. Though he had the feeling Sam might have said the same before he found his wife and a future he hadn't planned on.

Yet, oddly, there was a part of him that was almost

envious of his friend's good fortune as Ronan offered his hand. "Congratulations, though it's a frightening thought indeed, *you* a father."

"Ain't it just?" Sam shook his head and leaned down to brace his forearms on the cold metal railing in front of him. "I'll tell you flat out, never thought I'd be a family man."

Ronan could agree with that. Hell, it was one of the things that had cemented their friendship in the first place. The fact that neither of them believed in happily-ever-afters or, God help him, white picket fences. Now here they were, five years later and— "So what changed for you?"

"Honestly?" Sam turned dark brown eyes up to him. "Kara. She caught me off guard. Had me crazy for her and half out of my mind to have her before I knew what had happened." He shook his head and smiled in memory. "Before I knew it, I was hanging up my guns and opening this place to become a regular Joe."

Ronan laughed now. "Most regular Joes don't have shooting ranges in their backyards."

"All right," Sam conceded, "a *semi*-regular Joe. I've got my woman, got a company I'm proud of and a few good friends." He straightened up and slapped Ronan on the shoulder. "I call that lucky."

"Aye, you should." Ronan watched the trainees in silence for a few minutes before asking, "Are you planning on keeping the company then? With a pregnant wife, you're going to want to move closer to a town, wouldn't you?"

As if to emphasize his words, he stared off down the long road that led to the remote facility. It was five miles to the highway and then another thirty to the closest town. He wasn't exactly a family man, but the thought of being so far from help bothered even him.

"Been thinking about that," Sam admitted. "For now, we're good. Kara's healthy, and she loves it out here. She doesn't want to move, but I figure that might change once the baby comes. If it does, we'll go to six or seven two-week courses a year—and we'll live in town the rest of the time."

"Changes."

"Yeah, but life changes on you all the damn time whether you want it to or not."

So Ronan had seen for himself in the last few days and weeks. It was unsettling to a man who preferred order to chaos.

"And I don't," Ronan admitted with a shrug. "Never liked change much."

"No, you didn't," Sam said, laughing as they walked away from the training grounds, headed to the office. "I remember that time in Morocco when you…"

Ronan only half listened as his friend strolled down memory lane. Instead, he thought of Laura. He saw the happiness his friend had found and thought that maybe Sam had come out on top this time.

Four

Restless, Laura wandered her house, like a spirit looking for someone to haunt.

With Ronan gone, she should have been able to relax, let down her guard. Instead, she was more on edge than ever. Holding her coffee cup in one hand, she climbed the stairs and walked down the hall to Georgia's room. The door was open and Laura leaned on the doorjamb, looking in.

Georgia sat at her computer, a design program open to the interior of their condo—the living room specifically. While Laura watched, her sister used clicks of the mouse to change the wall colors and to digitally move the furniture around. She created wall hangings and rugs, changed the floor from wood to tile and when she was finished, Laura thought, the result was lovely.

"In the mood for a change?" Laura asked.

Georgia just smiled at the screen. "It's fun to experiment, but no. I think we're good for a while."

When she was married, Georgia had been an interior designer. But, when she divorced and moved back to California, Georgia had left everything of her old life behind. Including her dreams of a design studio of her own.

"Do you ever miss it?"

Sitting back in her chair, Georgia reached for her own cup of coffee, on the desk. She took a sip and made a face. "Yeesh. Gone cold." Setting it down again, she looked at Laura and admitted, "Sure I miss it sometimes, but I'm happier now. Working with you."

Funny, but neither of them were working at their dream jobs. If Laura had her way, she'd be making her living as an artist. But selling enough paintings to make a living was almost impossible. The real estate thing had happened because they both were good with people and someone always needed to buy a house. So she and Georgia both had put away the work they loved to do what they had to do. And if they bought the building for their business, then they would at least have that security behind them.

"Do you ever wish we could just—"

"Run away and join the circus?" Georgia finished for her with a grin.

"Something like that," Laura said.

"Who doesn't? Honey, most people don't get to spend their lives doing work they love. Most of them make do with good jobs that support their families."

"I know," Laura said with a sigh. "And I'm grateful that we have the work we do, don't get me wrong. But sometimes…"

"Yeah," her sister mused, with another glance at the design on the computer screen. "Sometimes."

Deliberately then, she shut off the program, grabbed her cup and stood up. "Come on, let's go downstairs and get me fresh coffee."

"We're crazy you know, drinking coffee this late. We'll both be up all night."

"Sleep is overrated," Georgia told her, stopping at the bottom of the stairs to give Beast a pat on the head.

It wasn't the sleeping that bothered Laura. It was the dreaming. Always of Ronan. She couldn't even close her eyes without seeing him.

In the kitchen, the bright, overhead light sent shadows scattering. Beyond the glass, the night was black and the skeletal limbs of the trees waved in the wind as if they were dancing.

"So, why can't *you* sleep?" Georgia asked, then corrected herself. "Why don't you *want* to sleep?"

"You know why," Laura said and took a seat at the kitchen table. Her reflection stared back at her from the window glass and she turned from it.

"Ronan." Georgia sat down opposite her and nodded. "I figured. He's been front and center for you since the moment you met him."

"I don't want him to be," Laura said.

"Too late for that."

Laura snorted. "True. Oh Georgia, this is all just a mess. Maybe Sean never should have brought Beast here. Then I never would have seen Ronan again and—"

"What's this Sean like anyway and why didn't I meet him?"

"You were out showing houses when Sean showed up here with Beast." Speaking of the dog made him appear. He wandered sleepily into the kitchen, strolled under the table and plopped down, his body covering both sisters' feet. Laughing a little, Laura said, "What's he like? Gorgeous, Irish and rich."

"Huh. A lot of that going around," Georgia murmured. "Why don't you go for him then? Forget Ronan and go for his cousin."

"Sure, good idea." Laura shook her head. "Way too late for that, too."

"Yeah, I suppose so." Georgia took a sip of her coffee. "It's a shame, really. I actually like Ronan. So if he hurts you again, I'm going to hate to have to get nasty."

"My hero," Laura said, smiling.

"Men may come and go," Georgia told her as she lifted her coffee cup in toast, "but sisters are forever."

"And I'm grateful, believe me." Laura shook her head and stared into her coffee cup as if looking for answers she couldn't find anywhere else. "I didn't mean for this to happen, you know? I didn't *want* to fall for him."

"I know, but really? Look at the man. Who could blame you?"

"So, what am I supposed to do about it?"

"Not much you can do, but wait it out," Georgia told her. "He left before, sweetie. He'll probably leave again."

Very true, Laura thought grimly. Ronan wasn't the kind to stay. She had known that going in and had thought she could deal with it. Well, she was wrong about that. And the longer he hung around now, the more her heart was engaged.

Probably a good thing that he was out of town for a bit. That would give her a chance to push him from her mind and wrap a little more metaphorical padding around her heart to try to protect it from the inevitable crushing.

* * *

He was gone for three days.

Laura didn't want to miss him, but she did. *Why* was the big question. She had spent the six weeks he was gone on that job convincing herself that it was for the best that they'd split up. She had allowed herself to feel too much for a man she knew was only temporary. And if they'd been together much longer, the pain of separation would have been that much harder to survive.

Yet, she couldn't seem to let go. Couldn't get him out of her mind. Couldn't even concentrate on work enough to stay settled, so early in the morning she grabbed her paints and headed to the beach.

That's where he found her.

She didn't have to hear him approach to know he was close by. Laura could *feel* his presence as surely as she would have a touch. Which only served to warn her of what she already knew: she was in deep trouble with no escape route.

"I went by the office, looking for you," he said, leaning casually against the iron railings that separated the greenbelt and sidewalk from the drop to the beach below.

"Yeah, I didn't go in today." Clearly. She didn't look at him. Instead, she kept her gaze locked on the ocean. After the stormy weather, the sky was a brilliant blue and the sea was still choppy, throwing up foam with every crashing wave against the shore.

"Georgia told me where to find you."

"So much for sisterly loyalty," she muttered with a quick glance at him. Oh, she wished she hadn't looked at him. He was wearing dark jeans, a thick, forest-green Irish sweater and the wind was tangling his hair just as she wanted to.

He smiled as if he knew what she was thinking. "I told her we had things to talk about."

"Do we?"

She was nervous. She hated that she was nervous. Her hand was shaking, so she took a tighter grip on her paintbrush and *willed* herself to even out. To get steady. No way would she let Ronan know how he affected her.

A few hardy surfers were out, looking for the perfect swell, but the sand was empty, and even the sidewalks were practically deserted. Not that many people interested in sitting out in a cold wind first thing in the morning. And a winter beach didn't attract many takers. Not even in southern California.

"You know we do," he said quietly.

"I know our conversations never go anywhere, and I'm too busy to run in circles today," she told him.

He moved away from the railing, walked around to stand behind her and look at the canvas that was nearly completed. She wasn't comfortable having anyone looking over her shoulder as she painted. Ronan only upped the nerve factor.

"I've no interest in circles, either," he said, lowering his head until his whisper sounded against her ear.

His breath on her skin was a sinful caress she sooo didn't need.

"Then go away."

"'Tis a public beach," he reminded her in that same, low whisper before he stood up and moved around her chair to block her view of the ocean.

"It is," she agreed. "And a big one. Why are you in my corner?"

"Because of you, Laura."

"So we're going to do the circle dance today anyway, are we?" she asked, hearing the snap in her tone and wincing at the sound of it. *Way to look unaffected, Laura.*

She wouldn't look at him again. Wouldn't meet his eyes. Because everything she was feeling would probably be written there for him to see. Ronan had always been too good at looking deeply. No doubt, exactly why he'd broken up with her in the first place.

He had seen that she was putting too much of herself into a relationship destined to end.

"Could you answer one thing for me?"

She risked another glance at him and felt her heart take a hard jolt. "Depends."

"Could you tell me why you sell real estate when you can paint like that?"

She stopped, lowered the brush she held in her right hand and took a long look at the nearly finished painting on her easel. It was good, she knew that. She had talent; every teacher she'd ever had had told her so. And she loved painting, though she didn't have as much time for it as she'd like.

"I like eating," she quipped and swept her brush across the painted sea. "Making a living from art isn't easy and real estate pays better. Well, usually."

"Seems a shame."

She didn't want his sympathy. "We do what we have to do, right?"

Seagulls wheeled and dipped in the sky, and the scent of coffee and sweet rolls drifted from a nearby diner. Laura took all of it in and none of it. Her eyes were focused on her painting, the rest of her was focused on Ronan. He slapped one hand against the metal railing, and she looked at him.

"We do," he said, "which is why I'm here."

"Ronan…"

His gaze was fixed on her. "You missed me."

"No, I didn't."

"Liar."

She frowned and lifted her gaze to his. Let him read what he would in her eyes, she wouldn't give him the satisfaction of admitting that he was right.

"I thought of you," he admitted and the Irish in his voice flavored every word. "Didn't want to, but I did."

A warm ball of satisfaction settled in the pit of her stomach, then slowly dissolved. "Didn't want to?"

He shook his head. "No, not on this trip or before, on the six-week job with that—"

"Singer?" she provided.

He grimaced. "Supposedly."

Laura smiled in spite of the still echoing twinge of knowing he hadn't wanted to think about her. "I actually saw you on TV one night. An entertainment show was covering her concert in Massachusetts and I caught a glimpse of you in the background." She didn't tell him that she'd heard nothing of the story because she had been too busy watching him. "You looked...uncomfortable."

"In pain is more like," he admitted, slapping the railing again for emphasis. "Between the girl and her mother, it was a long job."

She was glad to hear it. He'd broken up with her, then disappeared for six weeks. Helped to know that he was as miserable as she had been—even if for different reasons.

"Why did you go?" she asked. "Why take that job yourself?"

"It's what I do."

She shook her head and felt the wind slide through her hair, lifting it off her neck. "You told me yourself that you rarely take a guard job anymore. So why that one? To get away from me?"

After a moment's pause, he nodded. "I thought it best."

"To get over me."

"To let *you* get over *me*."

She laughed shortly. God, the man's ego was amazing. "Well, how thoughtful."

"I wasn't being thoughtful," he argued, the brogue in his voice thickening with irritation. "It was…necessary."

"For you," she said, picking up a new brush and dipping the edge of it into a splotch of white paint on her palette. When it was coated just thoroughly enough, she laid that white edge against the roiling swells on her painting. Instantly, the water looked more alive. More angry. Which, she supposed, was fair, since the artist herself was feeling pretty much the same.

"I didn't ask you to take care of me," she said.

"Perhaps not, but the request was there, toward the end of our time together, every time you looked at me, I saw it," he countered. "Thoughts and plans for a future that wouldn't be happening."

Maybe he had seen all of that in her eyes, Laura thought with a pang. But he'd sneaked up on her. She had thought what they shared was lust, pure and simple. A red-hot affair that would singe her socks off. She hadn't meant to feel for him. To fall for him. In fact, she had been determined *not* to feel anything remotely like what she had once thought she had with Thomas.

Back then, Laura had convinced herself she was in love because she had so badly wanted to be. She'd wanted a family. A home. Kids. Maybe she was an anachronism. A woman out of time. Most women were planning for big careers, chasing dreams and feeding their ambitions—and there was nothing wrong with that at all. But that just wasn't her.

Then, Georgia had been married, their parents off to Oregon, and Laura was alone. She had plenty of friends, but no…center. All she'd had was her condo and a job working for Manny Toledo—which was *no* woman's dream.

And then there was Thomas. Getting engaged had looked good on paper. But she'd been more in love with the idea of being in love than she had been with the oh-so-boring, predictable Thomas.

When he had cheated on her, she hadn't even really been mad. Or hurt. Or surprised. Which told her she had come close to making a huge mistake. Being lonely was one thing. Getting married for the wrong reasons was something else again.

Then Georgia's marriage ended, she moved in and suddenly, Laura wasn't as lonely anymore. She had her sister, her home and eventually, their own real estate business. It had been enough.

Until Ronan.

"So you wanted to save me from myself, is that it?" she asked thoughtfully. "So selfless."

"I was trying to make it easier," he countered. "On the both of us."

"Hmm. And how's that working for you?"

"Not bloody well at the moment," he admitted, shoving one hand through his windblown hair.

"Good to know," she muttered and dipped her brush into an open jar of turpentine. Then she used a rag to wipe it down before setting the brush aside for a more thorough cleaning when she got home.

No point in staying here any longer. She was losing the early morning light and Ronan's presence made it impossible to concentrate anyway. Methodically, she began putting away the tubes of oils, setting them in the mahogany box, each of them in their proper slots.

"You were right about something," he said after a long minute or two of silence.

Well, that got her attention. She looked up at him. "Really? About what?"

He frowned, shifted his gaze briefly to the crashing ocean behind him then turned his gaze back to her. "About Beast. I hadn't really thought about what would happen when it was time for me to go home."

Laura just stared at him. "The day you came to claim him, you told me you'd always planned on taking him to Ireland."

"Aye, well," he muttered as he scraped one hand across his face. "I may have exaggerated that point a bit."

Shaking her head, she twisted the lids onto her jars of turpentine and linseed oil, then slapped them both into the wooden case. "You lied."

"A bit," he agreed, "though it's no matter now anyway, because I *will* be taking him home."

He gave her a rueful smile that she should have found charming. Instead, she was simply annoyed.

"But I do admit," he continued, "that the thought hadn't occurred to me before you dog-napped him."

"I didn't—"

He held up one hand. "The point is, I got him at the pound because I missed having a dog about. I—"

"You were lonely?"

He narrowed his gaze on her and his jaw muscle twitched as if he were grinding his teeth. "I'm never lonely. 'Tis only that a house is an empty thing without a dog in it."

Ronan Connolly, billionaire bad-ass, would never admit to being lonely. But Laura could hear the real answer in his words. And it wasn't hard to understand. Thousands of miles away from his home, rattling around alone in that massive house on the cliffs of Laguna. No wonder he'd wanted a dog for the company.

"There I agree with you." She sighed and laid a piece of plastic wrap across the top of her palette, protecting the wet paint from smearing. Then she laid it carefully atop the paints stored inside the box, closed the lid and turned the lock.

"You'll still not give him back?"

"No." It was more now than protecting Beast from being ignored. Or about teaching Ronan that he couldn't walk away from a commitment. She loved Beast and as Ronan had just said himself, a house without a dog in it is an empty thing.

"Aye well, then I suppose we're not finished, you and I."

She stood up, folded her stool and leaned it against the trunk of a nearby tree. Taking her canvas down and setting it aside, she then collapsed the three-legged easel and laid it beside everything else. She didn't look up at Ronan until she was finished. When she did, she said, "No. I suppose not."

"You know what you're doing to me, don't you?" he asked suddenly.

"I'm not trying to do anything, Ronan."

"And that's just the frosting on the cake, isn't it? You don't even know it, and yet you still scramble my thoughts until I find myself here—" He took a breath. "As you said, talking in circles."

She hated that he could twist her insides into knots. Hated knowing that he didn't *want* to be anywhere near her—he was just too stubborn to leave before he had his answers.

And she was no better. She'd held off telling him. Giving him what he wanted from her because she hadn't been willing to see him walk away for good. But staring up into his eyes now, Laura knew that nothing would ever be as it was, so what the hell was she hanging on to? Ragged dreams? Tattered fantasies?

They were gone.

So for her sake, it was time to end this.

"You don't want to be here, so don't be."

He reached out for her, grabbed her shoulders and brought her to him. She felt the strength in his hands, read the determination in his eyes.

"Tell me," he insisted, drawing her even tighter to him. "Tell me what's driving you. What's kept that glint of banked fire in your eyes whenever you look at me. There's more going on here than just my dog—"

"This isn't about Beast," she said, temper flashing inside her like a struck match, billowing up in heat and flame. Laura pulled free of Ronan's grasp and staggered back a step or two.

"Then *what,* woman?"

She grabbed up her things, then spun around to face him. "You want to know what's eating at me, Ronan? Well, here it is. While you were off playing babysitter to that teenager, I was here at home, losing our baby."

He looked as if he'd been struck by lightning. His jaw dropped, his eyes went wide, then narrowed a heartbeat later. "You lost—"

"Now you know everything," she told him, lifting her chin and meeting those haunting eyes of his for what she knew would be the last time. "So goodbye, Ronan. Have a nice life."

She left him there, standing at the edge of the sea, and when she walked away, she didn't look back.

He followed her.

What else could he do?

Thoughts crashed through his mind with the wild ferocity of waves thundering against rocks. Blindly, he headed for his car and pulled into the street just moments behind Laura's Volkswagen. His hands fisted on the steering wheel, he was half surprised the damned thing didn't snap in his grip.

A child?

She'd lost their child and hadn't bothered to tell him?

What was he supposed to feel now? Relief? Grief? He didn't know. In a blur, his conversation with Sam came rushing home to him and Ronan saw it all so differently now. In a blink all had changed. He might have been a *father.* He could have been in Sam's shoes, waiting for the birth of a *child.* Shaken to the bone, he couldn't even separate the colliding emotions inside him. All he was sure of was the fury.

"Be damned if she'll simply lay something like that out, then leave me without so much as an explanation." He navigated Pacific Coast Highway, steering around the early morning traffic while his heart and guts twisted inside him until he could hardly draw a breath.

"A child, she says, then tells me it's gone?"

He made the turns as she did, keeping to the speed limit, watching carefully that he kept the anger inside him on a tight, short leash.

On her street, sunlight dappled through the trees planted on either side of the road. It was a pretty picture that he took absolutely no notice of. As she turned into the drive beside her house, he pulled his car up front and jumped out almost before the roar of the engine had died away. He came around the end of the car and stalked toward her, where she stood watching him as if he were a ghost.

Ronan laughed shortly. "That you can be surprised to see I followed you here amazes me. Did you really think it was ended? Because you said it was so?"

"You wanted your answer, you got it," she shot back, and reached into the car for her purse. When she went to get her painting supplies from the trunk though, Ronan stopped her with one hand on her arm. "Leave them till later."

He felt her tense in his grip, as if she'd fight him on this, then he felt resignation sweep that tension away. She turned her face up to his and through the anger in her eyes, he read a depth to her sadness he was stunned as hell to admit he hadn't noticed before. Had it been there since he got back? Had she been grieving the loss of his child without so much as mentioning it to him?

"Why the hell didn't you tell me you were pregnant?" he muttered, still lost in the gleam of sorrow shining back at him.

"When, Ronan? You were gone," she reminded him. "You made it clear you were done with me."

"If I'd known…" He let that sentence dangle for he wasn't sure even now what he might have done. How he might have reacted. Though he had damn well deserved the chance to make his own bloody decisions about how he felt.

"If you'd known," she said, "you would have thought I was trying to trap you into staying with me."

Maybe, he decided. Maybe he would have. And maybe not. "We'll not know for sure now, though, will we?"

"I know," she insisted and the grief in her eyes burned away in the flash of temper.

Was she right? He didn't want to think so, but a glimmer of something resembling shame rippled through him and he had to admit at least to the possibility. He hadn't planned on having a family. *Ever.* His own childhood had been enough of a roadmap to show him that emotional entanglements led to misery. Raised like that, Ronan was convinced he wouldn't have the slightest idea how to raise a child as it should be raised.

How could he show love to a child when he'd never seen it for himself?

And how could he grieve for a child he hadn't known existed until moments ago?

"Come on," he said, pulling her after him toward the house. "I'll not have this conversation out in the open."

She pushed her car door closed and hurried her steps to keep up with his much longer stride. "I don't want to do this now."

"That's a shame then, for sure." He drew her to a stop on the porch and held out one hand. "The key, Laura."

He could see the urge to argue in her eyes, but she only muttered something under her breath and handed over the keys she still held in her hand.

He had the door opened, her inside and the door slammed shut again in under a minute. Only then did he release the grip he had on her arm. He released her instantly, relieved to see he hadn't marked her fair skin, but damned if he had calmed down any. Standing feet braced widely apart, he barred the door with a stance that silently told her there would be no escape.

"Fine," she told him flatly. "We'll talk. Then you'll go."

Ronan sneered at her. She was already tossing him

out and he'd only just gotten in. "When I decide to go, I'll let you know."

"God, Ronan." She scooped one hand through the glory of her hair, lifting it up off her neck before letting it fall down in waves around her shoulders again. "There's nothing more to tell."

"Oh, aye, there is," he said and even he heard his brogue thickening with the temper clawing at the base of his throat. "You tell me *my* child lived and died inside of you before I even knew of it and you think there's nothing more to be said?"

A sheen of tears filled her eyes and Ronan was slightly horrified. He knew if she cried, he would lose this fine edge of temper. He couldn't stand a woman crying. Made him feel helpless. Or big and clumsy, and none of those were attributes he normally assigned to himself.

"Don't do that," he ordered and watched her flinch at his tone. He felt a right bastard and quickly added, "And don't do that, either."

She sniffed, jerked up her head and fired a hot glare at him that should have singed the ends of his hair. "What *should* I do then, oh Master of the Universe?"

Sarcasm aside, he much preferred fire in her eyes than the sorrow that grated at the edges of his heart.

"Tell me more. All of it." He tore his gaze from hers, scraped both hands over his face and fought for some of that legendary Connolly control. But by damn, he felt as if his legs had been cut out from under him. When he knew he could speak without issuing another bloody order, he said, "I've a need to know, Laura."

When his gaze shifted back to hers, he saw her nod and blow out a breath. "All right. All right. A few weeks after you ended things, I found out I was pregnant."

Something inside him quaked again, but he steadied himself. Though this was still hard to wrap his head around, because if there was one thing Ronan was sure of, he *always* took precautions. He didn't risk making a child with a woman who wouldn't be permanent in his life.

And since *no* woman would be permanent in his life, a child was out of the question. "We used condoms."

She snorted and wrapped both arms around her middle. "That's what I told myself after I took the pregnancy test. Then I read the package. Ninety-seven percent effective."

Grimly, he swallowed that information. "And do they bury that bit of news in the fine print?"

"Nope, right on the front."

"Well, that's a hell of a thing." He waved that information away as unimportant and urged her on. "You found you were pregnant and you didn't tell me because—"

"Because you'd already made it clear you didn't want me." A flush of color in her cheeks told him that their breakup still stung and he could have kicked himself. He'd been so damned sure that he was doing the right thing for the right reasons and still he'd managed to foul everything up somehow. Now, he told himself, he was paying the price for it.

"Fine—then what?"

"Then you left on your bodyguard job. You told me the night you broke up with me that you'd be going—"

"And you didn't bother to think that a change of circumstance might require a phone call?" He couldn't keep silent on this because—oh, how it raged at him. She hadn't told him. He hadn't known he had created a life until it was gone and that was something that would haunt him.

"I did call."

His gaze narrowed on her. "What? When?"

"A week or so into your job," she said and turning away from him, walked into the narrow living room. He watched her go, her steps clicking softly against the wooden floor. She headed for the overstuffed couch with a bold print pattern and when she reached it, she dropped like a stone into the corner of the thing. Grabbing up a throw pillow in sunshine yellow, she hugged it to her chest and looked up at him through blue eyes that looked bruised with memory.

"I called when I went to the hospital."

He would have remembered that. "Laura—"

"I did," she insisted. "Your cell was turned off, and I couldn't leave a message—not *that* message anyway—so I called Cosain and talked to Brian. Your assistant. He told me he'd call you and have you get in touch with me." She sighed. "You never did. Your meaning came through loud and clear, Ronan. No worries. I didn't call again. I didn't bother you with what I was going through." She took a long, deep breath as if to steady herself, then her gaze fixed on his, she said quietly, "And now I want you to leave."

He hardly heard her. He was thinking, realizing the truth of what she said. The memory was there, Ronan thought in regret. Brian's call, telling him that Laura was trying to reach him.

He hadn't called her back. Had told himself it was too soon after their end for them to speak again.

That she was still hungering for him. That she was trying to win him back and though it had been a nice stroke on the ego, he'd been worried that talking to her would only tempt him to pick up where they'd left off. Ah, God.

"You remember," she said. "Brian did call you."

"Aye, he did." He pushed one hand through his hair, tugging as he went and the sharp sting of pain cleared the fog in his mind.

"And you did nothing."

"I didn't know, did I?" And as that thought settled into his brain, he assured himself that if he had known the truth, of course he would have called her. Hell, he'd have come back from the road to be with her. He'd have done...*something*.

But she didn't give him the chance. She took that from him. From them.

"You didn't want to know, Ronan." She tossed the pillow to one side, and stood up. Kicking her shoes off she stalked barefoot across the floor, headed to the front door. Her head up, hair flying like a honey-colored flag in her wake, she said, "Now that you know it all, you can go. And don't come back this time, Ronan. We really are done now."

He stopped her as she passed him. It was instinct more than anything else that had him reaching for her, grabbing hold of her arm and turning her to look at him.

"You can say that to me? That easily? We're done, our child is gone and goodbye?"

She pulled free of him, and the temper he much preferred to her pain flashed in her eyes. "You don't get to say that to me. You're the one who said goodbye and walked away, Ronan. And our child was hardly more than a wish when I lost it."

At those last words, her bottom lip trembled a bit until she made the effort to firm it, for which he was grateful.

He reached out and set both hands on her shoulders, forcing her to be still. To stand there and meet his eyes. Hear him. "I'd have been here, Laura, had I known."

"I think I believe you," she said. "But it's probably better that you weren't. Really. You were right to go when you did. It's pointless to pretend that we had more than a few months of sex and fun."

"We almost had more," he argued, his voice gentle, unsure still of what he was feeling.

"And what would that have meant? That you would be with someone you didn't want because of a child you hadn't planned on?"

She shook her head sadly and gave him the worst excuse for a smile Ronan had ever seen. "No, better this way. As hard as it was, as hard as it is to say, it's better this way."

"It's not," he said, pulling her closer as his gaze moved over her face, from the haunted pools of her eyes to the slope of her mouth and the tip of her tongue as she smoothed it across her bottom lip. "*This* is better."

His mouth claimed hers and hunger exploded between them.

Five

Laura's insides lit up like a sudden lightning flash. Every cell in her body was electrified, buzzing with sensation, with heat. She leaned into him, even knowing that she shouldn't. That this wasn't the answer to anything. But a staggering weight was off her shoulders now that she had finally shared the secret that had been haunting her for weeks. It felt so good to be held by him again.

It had been too long.

And she'd *missed* him.

His hands moved up and down her back, cupped her behind, then slid up again as if he was reacquainting himself with the feel of her. As if he had to remap every curve to his satisfaction.

That so worked for her.

How could she be furious with him one second and the next only want him on her, *in* her? It made no sense, and it didn't seem to matter. There was something about Ronan Connolly that had punched every one of her buttons from the first time she saw him.

He tightened his arms around her until he was a vise, holding her in place, though she didn't mind because there was nowhere else she'd rather be. His tongue tangled with hers, his breath became hers. She opened for him, taking as well as giving and needing so much more.

Her knees felt like they were dissolving, but she didn't need them because he was there, holding her up. Laura's mind blurred. Happened every time he kissed her. Only he had ever caused this wild scramble of brain cells. Only he could make her crazy with a kiss. The man had a serious mouth on him and knew how to use it.

In the one small corner of her mind that was still rational, still cogent, a voice whispered that this was a mistake. That she shouldn't go back down this road. But Laura wasn't interested in logic.

Later maybe, she'd come to regret this. But for now, all she wanted was Ronan. He knew now what she'd been feeling, and she could sense that he felt at least some of her pain over what had been lost. Taking comfort from each other, losing themselves in the magic they made together felt…right.

She'd craved him for weeks and now that he was here, she couldn't turn her back on her own needs. Her own desires.

"Now," he whispered when he tore his mouth from hers only to trail his lips and tongue along the column of her throat. "I need you."

"Oh, me, too. Want you, now." She threaded her fingers through his thick hair and held his head to her neck, loving the feel of him pressed against her. His hot breath puffing against her skin. She wanted more. All of it. Wanted the sensations only he could cause, and wanted them to go on and on.

"Let's go, then." He bent, swept one arm under her legs and lifted her off her feet in one easy move.

Laura wasn't dainty. Nor petite. No man before him had ever picked her up and, ridiculous or not, it was a gesture romantic enough to send her heartbeat into a wild gallop.

He knew where her bedroom was. God knew he'd been there often enough—before.

In the hallway, sunlight speared through the skylight overhead, laying out a golden path that would lead directly to her bed. As he stalked down the sun-dazzled oak floor, his steps echoed out around them and sounded to Laura's fuzzed out brain, like the hands of a clock, sweeping toward inevitability. He carried her through the open door to her room and stopped dead.

"Useless," he murmured on a laugh.

Laura followed his gaze and couldn't stop her own laugh. Her fierce guard dog was in the middle of her bed, flat on his back, all four legs jutting into the air so that he looked like road kill.

"Easy to see why you want such a magnificent animal," Ronan said softly, a smile curving his incredible mouth.

"He has his good points," she argued in defense of Beast.

"None of which I'm interested in at the moment," he told her, then spoke louder. "Beast, you lazy sod, off the bed!"

The dog opened his eyes and turned his head to look at them. A tail wag his only other response.

"He's tired, poor baby," Laura said, as her fingers slid through Ronan's hair.

"Maybe so, but he's in me way," Ronan argued. "Go on now. Go sleep on the couch, you great lump of fur."

With an all too human-sounding sigh, the dog rolled over, jumped off the bed and left the room, pausing only to give them both an offended glare.

Ronan stepped into the room, slammed the door behind them, then carried Laura to the bed and dropped her on the mattress. "Never thought to fight a dog for space in your bed."

"No fight necessary," she told him and lifted both arms in welcome.

Ronan was there, in her arms a heartbeat later, his big, warm body covering hers, his mouth on hers again, stoking the slow-burning embers inside into a conflagration big enough to char them both.

Then he rolled over, until she was lying on top of him, and once he had her there, he scooped his big hands beneath the hem of her sweater and tugged it up and over her head. She wore a T-shirt beneath and, in a moment, that was gone, too. Only her bra remained and Ronan's magic fingers undid the front clasp and then pushed it off her arms to be tossed to the floor with the rest.

"Ah, lovely," he whispered and Laura *felt* lovely as his hands cupped her breasts. His thumbs rubbed across her sensitive nipples until she moaned gently at the quiver inside her.

"So good," she said softly, reaching up to cover his hands with her own.

"I didn't want to miss you, damn it," Ronan told her, and Laura knew she should be angry at hearing it. Then she realized what he was saying and she held the words inside her in a quiet, dark spot so she could pull them out later and feel them again.

It was a kind of power, she thought as she stroked

her hands up and down his forearms, felt the crisp, dark hairs against her palms. To know that he wanted her in spite of himself.

"I wanted you to miss me, Ronan. Wanted you to be miserable because you walked away." She reached down for the hem of his green sweater and tugged it up, with him shifting to help her yank it off of him. His shirt was gone an instant later, and she slid her palms across his hard, muscled chest, loving the heat of his body pouring into hers.

He hissed in a breath and stared into her eyes. "You got your wish then," he ground out, "for I did miss you." He lifted his hands to cup her face. "I did want you and hated every moment I was away from you. Is that enough?"

"Not nearly," she confessed and lowered her head to kiss him.

He clutched her tight, rolled again on the bed until he was levered over her. Then he stripped the rest of her clothes from her, tossing them to the floor, leaving her lying naked in a slant of sunlight across the mattress.

She watched him, breath hitching in her chest, as he stood and tore his own clothes off. Her gaze swept him up and down and everything inside her jittered as if lightning had struck her again. Then he was back with her, his body sliding over hers, the hard, thick need of him pressing into her, letting her know just how much he wanted her.

A damp, aching heat settled at her center and throbbed in time with her fluttering heartbeat as they rolled across the bed, wrapped tightly in each other's arms. Hands explored, mouths worshipped, sighs and groans slid into the sun-warmed air and hung there, sizzling from the combined heat of lovers too long apart.

Laura's pulse raced. Each breath came short and sharp. He touched her and she burned, he stopped touching her and she ached.

He slid one hand to the apex of her thighs and cupped her, holding tight as she instinctively rocked her hips into his touch. As she groaned and writhed in a kind of panicked need she'd never known before.

"Ronan—"

"I love touching you," he whispered, dipping his head into the curve of her neck and shoulder. "The hot feel of you moving against me. The sigh of your breath. The scent of you." He raised his head, looked down into her eyes and muttered thickly, "I missed it all. Missed *you*."

He pushed first one finger, and then two, deep inside her and Laura's mind splintered a little. She grabbed at his shoulders and clung to him. Her hips moved in the rhythm he set with his deep caresses. His thumb rubbed over one incredibly sensitive spot until she actually heard herself whimper his name in desperation.

"I'll have you now, Laura. As you'll have me."

"Yes," she said, swallowing hard, fighting for breath, "now, Ronan. Please, now."

He kissed her again, long and hard and deep, tangling his tongue with hers in a frantic dance that only served to drive the ache inside her higher and higher.

When he pulled back from her, she wanted to cry out and bit her lip to keep that secret to herself.

"Condoms," he blurted. "For all the good they do, are they still here, in the drawer?"

"Yes. Yes."

He moved away and she heard the drawer open and shut.

"Hurry, Ronan!"

"Aye. I am."

She watched him tear a condom free and sheathe himself and it was all she could do to keep from reaching for him, doing it herself, just so she could touch him. Indulge herself in the wonder of wrapping her fingers around him.

But the moment passed and he was back, kneeling between her parted thighs, staring down at her as if she were the last steak at a beggar's banquet. When she met his fevered gaze, she saw raw passion glittering in his eyes. Sunlight streamed across him, catching red tones in his hair and gilding his flesh with a light that made him seem almost unreal. A fantasy.

And for now anyway…he was *hers*.

"Come here to me," he said and sat back on his haunches as he took her hands and pulled her up against him.

She straddled him, he took hold of her hips and lowered her inch by tantalizing inch onto the hard length of him.

Laura's head fell back. A deep-throated groan ripped from her as he invaded her slowly, exquisitely, drawing out the pleasure/torture for both of them. She wanted him fast and hard but this…lingering…was too good to ignore.

When at last she had claimed all of him and he was seated deep inside her, she lifted her head to meet his gaze. She bent her head and took his mouth, teeth tugging at his bottom lip. Sparks flared in his eyes and she felt an answering shower of fire inside her.

Slow wasn't enough. Tender wasn't what they needed. In unspoken agreement, he tossed her back onto the bed and followed her down, his body still linked with hers.

She lifted her legs and hooked her ankles at the small of his back. He moved inside her, his hips pistoning suddenly as if he'd held himself on a tight leash as long as he could and now he would claim what he needed. What *they* needed.

She relished it. The slap of flesh to flesh, the sound of his breath coming faster and faster. The push and pull of his body slamming into hers. She moved with him, against him, and the coil of heat inside her expanded until she felt as though she might drown in it. And she didn't care.

This was what she had waited for. What she had ached for the whole time they were apart. This…magic that she found only with Ronan. He was it for her and had been from the first. Ronan Connolly and the things he could do to her.

Again and again, they crashed together, each of them fighting for the release that hovered just out of reach.

Her hands swept up and down his back, reveling in the feel of him beneath her palms. Then she moved to cup his face, slide her hands down his neck over his shoulders, across his chest. He hissed in air at her every stroke, and she shivered to know what she could do to him.

What they could make between them.

Tension coiled deep and suddenly exploded. When the first climax took her, Laura shouted his name and clung to him as wave after wave of pleasure shattered her heart. Her soul.

She held him when his own body erupted and with a shout of triumph, Ronan leapt into oblivion, still holding her tightly to him. Laura cradled him close as, wrapped together, they tumbled blindly into the fire.

For a minute or two, Ronan was almost afraid he'd been struck blind. Then he realized he had collapsed on top of Laura and his head was buried in the tangle of her hair. She smelled so damn good, he didn't want to lift his head, but still, he did, looking down into eyes that were at once energized and slumberous.

"I'm crushing you," he murmured, and went up on one elbow. His body still locked inside hers, he was in no hurry to disentangle them. The feel of her surrounding him was too damned good to give up just yet.

"I don't feel crushed," she said, stroking one finger along the center of his chest.

Fire trailed in the wake of her touch and he idly wondered how he could be shaking from his release only to be craving another?

She lay in the sun like a fallen goddess, all light and golden, her hair a fall of honey across the blue duvet on her bed. She was warm and sexy and he wanted her all over again. But there were things to talk about. And Ronan wasn't a man to put off the inevitable.

"I didn't come here for this, you know," he started and watched her eyes shadow, as if a chill was leaching away the warmth.

"I know. I didn't mean for this to happen, either." She gave his chest a gentle push and he took her meaning, reluctantly separating himself from her.

Already a distance was forming between them, and though he knew that for the best, it didn't make it any easier to abide.

"Damn it Ronan, you shouldn't have followed me home."

"I was to simply let you walk away after telling me—"

"Fine. Fine. That was my fault," she grumbled. "I hadn't meant to tell you at all. And certainly not in that way, but you just made me so mad..."

"Well, I know the feeling," he said and his smile faded when she didn't return it.

How had this gone from heat and fire to cold and ice so quickly? he wondered. He'd felt the rightness of it when he was inside her. And now, it was as though they were different people, standing on opposite sides of a wall that only got higher the longer they were together.

The hell of it was, he wanted her still.

Before he could say such a stupid thing aloud, he made for the bathroom and when he came back, she was still sitting on the bed, still gloriously naked, and for that, he was grateful. If he couldn't touch, he could at least look. And really, what would be the point in covering herself up when they'd only just been as close as two people could be?

He walked back to her bed and sat down beside her. "We've things we should talk about."

She sighed and pushed her heavy fall of hair back behind her shoulders. "If this is another goodbye speech, I'll skip it, thanks just the same."

A twist of temper lodged in the center of his chest, but he deliberately smothered it. "Not a speech, damn it. I've only just learned I was to be a father. I don't even know what to think of that. How to feel."

"It's over, Ronan. It didn't happen. You don't have to say anything to me about it."

"I do," he insisted. "I just don't know *what*."

Infuriating to not know. He was accustomed to being in control. To having the upper hand. And in this, he hadn't a clue. He was as lost here as he might have been if someone had dropped him in the middle of Kansas.

"Then let me," she said and scooted off the bed, as if she needed physical as well as emotional distance from him.

She walked to the bathroom, plucked her robe off the back of the door and slipped the sapphire blue, satin garment on, tying it at the waist. The fact that the material gaped enough to give him a glimpse of one creamy breast was something he was sure she wasn't aware of.

"I've had a lot of time to think about this. About *us*," she said, walking toward him, but stopping a few feet from him. "If I hadn't lost the baby, we would have had a connection between us forever, Ronan."

"And a marriage," he told her flatly.

She was surprised at that; he saw it in her eyes. She waved it away though and said, "Doesn't matter now anyway, but my point is, there is no baby. So there is no connection, Ronan. We're just two people who happen to be really great in bed together."

He wasn't sure why he felt he'd been insulted, but the sting was there nonetheless.

"There's more."

"Is there?" She laughed and shook her head. "No, there isn't, and you don't have to pretend for me. You left because you didn't want more."

"That's not entirely the way of it," he insisted, though a voice inside told him she had it *exactly* right.

"Ronan." She stepped closer, stopping close enough for him to reach out and grab hold of her, but he didn't because her eyes were still cool, dispassionate.

"Ronan, when I lost the baby, it made me realize something important."

"Aye? And what's that?"

She smiled and gave a little shrug that dipped the fabric of her robe even more. Almost enough to expose one pink nipple. His insides fisted in response.

"I *want* a family. Children. A husband. Forever."

He gritted his teeth and slipped off the bed, moving

past her to grab up the clothes he'd torn off just moments before.

"Don't look so worried," she said on a choked off laugh. "I'm not nominating you for the position of husband."

"Laura—" He looked at her and it took every ounce of his will not to go to her, snatch her up and toss her back onto the bed, where everything between them made sense.

"I said I want a husband. I didn't say *you* were the guy."

Maybe she hadn't said it, he told himself, but she had thought it at one point or another in their time together. He'd seen it in her eyes.

"I'm not," he assured her, "though if I were…"

"No ifs," she told him. "I don't need you to placate me. Or to patronize me. I just need you to understand that this…" she waved a hand at the rumpled bedclothes behind her "…won't happen again. I'm not made for affairs. That's just not who I am. I thought I could do it, have sex with you and keep it simple. But nothing about you is simple, Ronan."

"Doesn't sound like a compliment," he said, tugging his jeans on.

"Didn't mean it as one." She walked to him and when she was close enough, she went up on her toes and kissed him, just a slight brush of her lips to his. Then she stepped back, tightened the belt of her robe and swung her hair back from her face. "*That's* goodbye, Ronan. Whatever we had together died along with our baby."

What the bloody hell could he say to that without sounding like a moron?

He'd come here full of fire and righteous fury and

he'd leave here satisfied in body and muddled of mind. Did all women have this ability to wreak havoc on a man?

Or was it just Laura?

He looked into her blue eyes and read regret shining there, along with the goodbye she'd just proclaimed. And he knew, that for today at least, they were done.

Six

The stone patio felt rough, cold and damp against his bare feet. He wore only jeans, hitched low on his hips. The icy wind pushed at him from the sea as if slapping at him. Ronan didn't mind. He needed the cold. It made him sharp. Cleared out the fog in his mind and the heaviness inside him.

He lifted one hand to rub his fist against the center of his chest, in a futile effort to ease the ball of ice settled there. Taking a long pull on his beer, Ronan walked to the edge of the patio, dropped one hand to the wood railing and stared out to sea.

The waves rolled in and crashed on the cliffs below. Moonlight skittered in and out from behind a bank of clouds and intermittently turned the surface of the ocean to a bright silver. From next door came the muted sounds of a stereo and there was a distant hum of traffic from the highway above and behind the house.

His fist tightened around the long neck of the beer bottle and his eyes narrowed even further as he looked not at the scene in front of him, but at his own memories of the day.

Since the moment Laura had dropped her bomb on him that morning, nothing had made sense.

Which was the problem, he thought grimly, taking another long drink of his beer. Following Laura home, ending up in her bed, hadn't steadied him. If anything, it had only fed the imbalance he felt. As if the world as he knew it had been cut out from under him. As if the stones beneath his feet were no more substantial than the insistent wind tearing at his hair.

A child.

Laura had been pregnant. With *his* child. And it was gone. How was he to deal with that? He saw her again, in memory, standing beneath the shade of a tree, spilling her secret, and he standing there like the village idiot, as if he hadn't a mind to think or a tongue to speak the words crowding his mouth. But what could he say?

He still didn't know what to think of it. But he knew what he thought of what had happened after. The slow boil of Laura facing him down and telling him goodbye. The coolness of her gaze. The polite, distant tone of her voice. She'd shut him out. Shut him down. As bloodlessly, he was forced to admit, as he had shut her down a couple of months ago.

"But this is different," he insisted to the shadows crouched at the edges of his patio.

How it was different didn't matter. What mattered was that *no* woman had ever walked away from Ronan Connolly before today and damned if he was going to let Laura be the first.

"Be damned if I will," he assured himself, words snatched away by the wind as soon as they were uttered.

There was more between them yet to be settled. The electrifying heat when they came together was still there, so they weren't finished with each other. Not at all. He'd let her go too early. His mistake.

"But I can fix that." A slow smile curved his mouth as he lifted his beer for another sip. And standing in the wind-tossed darkness, a plan built in his mind.

Laura's eyes were gritty and her head was pounding from lack of sleep.

So when Ronan walked into the real estate office, she took a deep breath and held it, half hoping she'd simply pass out. She was in no way ready for another confrontation with the man who had invaded her thoughts all night.

Heck, if she tried—which she wouldn't—she would still be able to feel his hands on her. Feel the hot, thick slide of his body into hers and—

Oh, God.

"Uh-oh," Georgia muttered, loud enough that Laura heard her from across the room.

Ronan's lips quirked, which told her that he, too, had heard Georgia. Great. Just fabulous.

Still, she couldn't blame her sister, since Georgia had been Laura's sounding board all morning while she raged about Ronan and figuratively kicked herself for going to bed with him again.

"Good morning, ladies," Ronan announced, Ireland singing in his voice. His gaze swept the room in an instant, as if to assure himself that no one but the Page sisters were in the office.

He looked good, she thought, which was completely

unfair. If she'd been awake all night, unable to sleep, then he, too, should look haggard and irritable. But no, in his black jeans, thick Irish sweater and his hair carelessly wind-tossed, he looked more like he had stepped off the cover of a magazine.

She frowned up at him when he crossed to her desk, planted both hands on the sleek wood surface and leaned in.

"We have to talk," he announced.

"Um, I think I'll go for coffee," Georgia said, jumping up from her desk like she'd been shot.

"Don't you dare," Laura warned, fixing her sister with a glare designed to keep her in place. There was simply no way she was going to be alone with Ronan this morning. She was still too...affected by their time together last night. The sad truth was, she didn't trust herself with him just now.

Her mind might be coolly logical about keeping him at a distance, but her body had other, more interesting ideas.

"Is there something you needed?" she asked, looking up into those amazing blue eyes of his.

One corner of his mouth tipped up. "Well, now, an interesting question."

Laura cringed. She'd walked into that one. "Ronan, we're busy." She picked up a manila file folder from her desk as if to drive that point home.

"As am I, Laura," he assured her, pushing up from the desk and shoving his hands into his pockets. "'Tis why I'm here."

Across the room, Georgia was making faces at her and jerking her head as if to shout, *For heaven's sake, just talk to the man.*

Easy for her to mime.

Laura inhaled sharply and said, "Ronan we said all we had to say yesterday. You have the answers you wanted, so why are you here now?"

"Oh," he assured her with a wink, "I've not learned nearly enough. But I'm here on another matter entirely. This visit isn't personal, Laura. 'Tis business."

Business? Georgia mouthed.

Laura ignored her sister and focused on the man in front of her. Lord knew it was no hardship to look at him. But when she caught the gleam in his eyes, she started to worry.

"I've come for your services—" he smiled at her "—your services professionally speaking, of course. I want you to find me a house to buy."

For one heart-stopping second, she was excited at the thought. She'd helped him find places to rent both for his business and his residence when she first met him. But he hadn't been looking to buy then, wanting to take his time and scope out the area.

Her commission on the kind of home Ronan would be interested in buying would be enormous. More than enough for a down payment on their building, a voice in her mind whispered. Too bad, she thought, that he wasn't serious. He was up to something, she knew, and it had nothing to do with buying a house.

"No," she argued, in spite of the way her sister was tugging at her hair in frustration. "You don't want to buy a house, Ronan. You're trying to drag me into some kind of game, and news flash—I'm not going to play."

He was only interested in making her crazy, and the way her head was spinning and her blood humming, she had a feeling he was well on his way to succeeding.

He gave her a frown, pulled his hands from his pockets and crossed his arms over his chest. "I've no interest in games, Laura. I'm here as a buyer and I'm willing to start the looking now. Are you so willing to turn away my business for the sake of your pride?"

"My *pride?*" She slowly rose to her feet so she could meet him glare for glare. "You think this is about my pride?"

"What other reason could it be? Unless of course you don't trust yourself with me…"

She actually *saw* red. Her vision blurred and temper had her heartbeat jittering frantically. Just because she'd been thinking only moments ago that she didn't really trust herself to be alone with him was no reason for *him* to think it. The man's ego was enormous.

"Laura…" Georgia was jabbing a finger at the doorway to the office kitchenette, no doubt wanting to talk about this.

Laura shook her head.

Ronan hid a smile, but not before she saw it. He was enjoying himself, damn it.

He spoke again, and Laura glanced at her sister in time to see Georgia clutching her throat as if she were choking.

"The cliff house is fine for a rental," Ronan was saying, "but I want something permanent."

Her eyes narrowed on him in suspicion. "Why? You'll be going back to Ireland."

One dark brown eyebrow lifted. "And spending plenty of time here as well. Cosain is growing. I'll need to have a base in California as well as in Ireland."

Laura dropped one hand to the phone on her desk and clicked her fingernails against the back of it in a rapid tempo that mimicked what her heartbeat was doing. When his gaze dropped to her nervous fingers, she stilled them.

Torn between the temptation of a huge commission and the urge to throw him out, Laura could only stare at him. She was angry, too. He couldn't get to her any other way, so now he'd decided to wave a check at her.

"You use your money to get what you want?"

His gaze narrowed on her. "Is there a reason I shouldn't? And is it, Laura, that you don't so much have a problem with me offering it as you do with yourself wanting to take it?"

"I don't like being bought."

"I'm buying a house, not you."

She flushed, temper rising. He had her, damn it, and he knew it. Laura couldn't afford to be offended. She and Georgia needed that money to set their own world right and turning it down would cost her sister. Not something Laura was prepared to do.

He would know that, too, the bastard. When they first got together, they'd spoken of their families. He knew how close she and Georgia were. How they were struggling. He hadn't, he'd said at the time, been able to empathize, as the only family he had were his cousin Sean and Sean's mother. But he could sympathize.

Now, he was using what he knew against her and doing it damned well, too.

Silence spun out in the room for several long moments and hung there, caught in a web of tension so thick Laura could hardly draw a breath. Neither of them shattered the spell. It was Georgia who finally spoke up.

"If you want my opinion," she said.

"Really don't," Laura snapped.

"Well, I'd be interested," Ronan said.

Georgia didn't need much encouragement. Ronan smiled as she came around her desk and walked across the room to stand beside him. She barely looked at him though, keeping her gaze fixed on her sister.

"Are you nuts?" she asked.

Laura heard Ronan's snort of laughter as she said, "Excuse me?"

"Well, come on," her sister said, "business isn't great enough to turn down any prospective buyer."

"He isn't a buyer," Laura argued. "He's using his money to manipulate me. *Us.*"

"*Manipulate's* a harsh word," he insisted. "I need a house. You sell houses. Seems simple enough to me."

"There you go! It's settled." Georgia took Laura's arm and pulled her up from her chair. "So why don't you two head out for some coffee? Ronan can tell you what he's thinking of and meanwhile I'll print out some likely prospects in the Laguna area. You like the cliffs, right?"

"I do. Reminds me of home."

"Great, good." Georgia picked up Laura's purse and handed it to her. "So go on now, I should have ten or twenty listings for you by the time you get back."

"They shoot traitors, you know," Laura murmured.

"Hey, it's Tuesday," Georgia said, herding Laura and Ronan to the door. "Carmen always makes cinnamon rolls on Tuesdays. You can bring me back one."

Ronan was on the street in the sunshine blinking a moment later, thinking that Georgia would have made an excellent bodyguard. She took charge, and apparently, since she had ignored her sister's fury, the woman was fearless as well.

"You use your money like a club," Laura said hotly. "Have you ever noticed that?"

"It's not a club, but, aye, I have used it as a weapon before. And will again." He used what he had to win. Always had. Always would.

"You seem proud."

"Why wouldn't I be?" He stepped onto the sidewalk after her. "I've got it. What good is it to stand about and *not* use it?"

"You don't play fair."

"I play to win and you know that very well," he said, catching her gaze with his.

She blew out a breath. "Are you serious about this?" Laura asked, tucking her purse under her left arm.

"I am," he said. Dead serious. This was the perfect plan. After all, he would need a house here. He despised renting and hotels didn't suit him. And the added benefit to the protracted house hunt he had in mind was the time Laura would be forced to spend with him.

He wasn't done. Not by a long shot. The knowledge that this woman had actually carried and lost his child had still not completely sunk in. But if she thought the connection between them was severed, she was wrong. She wouldn't be turning her back on him. Locking him out of her life. Her bed. Not yet, anyway.

Damned if he would be tossed aside. The explosive sex they'd shared the night before had only served to convince him that he'd made a mistake in ending what was between them so soon. He wanted her. She wanted him. He'd have her back in his bed, where she belonged, and when he finally decided he'd had enough, then and only then, would they be over.

She watched his eyes as if searching for a trick, a trap. But she would find nothing there he didn't want her to see. He knew well how to keep his own secrets.

Finally, Laura nodded and started walking. "Fine, then. We'll go have coffee, talk about what you want and then I'll take a poisoned cinnamon roll back to my sister."

He laughed and she shot him a wry grin. "Okay, not poisoned."

"Is it so hard then, Laura, to work with me?"

"Not if that's all you want from me." Her red heels made a pleasant clicking sound against the sidewalk. "I am a professional, after all."

"Exactly what I was thinking," he told her, and took one moment to indulge himself in admiring her. That thick, blond hair hung in a tumble of waves past her shoulders. She wore a red blazer with a white shirt and black skirt that stopped a few inches above her knees. A lovely woman with a glint in her blue eyes that told him whatever he had in mind, she was ready for it.

They'd just see about that.

"Gets busy early around here." He took her arm and pulled her to one side as a skateboarder hurtled past them, earphones in his ears, head rocking to music only he could hear.

"Just like anywhere else," Laura said. "Businesses are open and hopefully people come out to buy."

Traffic jostled for space on this narrow section of Pacific Coast Highway. Pedestrians darted through the stopped cars, unwilling to walk to the crosswalk or wait for a green light. Sunlight poured down on the entire scene from a bright blue sky and from somewhere up ahead, the scent of fresh baked goods wafted to them on the sea wind.

Laura took a deep breath and sighed. "Tuesdays at Carmen's can't be beat." Then she looked up at him. "Come on then, we'll snag a table and talk—about business."

"Wouldn't have it any other way," he said and smiled to himself when she turned to walk on.

Surfers, children and an elderly couple were waiting

patiently in line. Ronan insisted on placing the order and sent Laura off to find them a table in the already crowded bakery.

She was waiting for him at a corner spot by the front window. The tables were small and round and the tiny chairs were not built for a man of Ronan's size. But he made do, being sure to bump his knees against Laura's as he took his seat.

"Your friend does good business here."

Laura took the plastic lid off her latte and blew gently across the surface before taking a sip. "She makes superior cinnamon rolls. Among other things."

He took a bite and had to agree as sugar and spice dissolved into heaven on his tongue. Ronan hadn't even realized he was hungry, but now he practically inhaled the pastry and gave Laura a sheepish grin when she asked, "Hungry, are we?"

"I'm a man of many appetites," he told her and had the pleasure of watching her flush.

"Okay," she said flatly. "First rule. No flirting."

"I don't flirt."

"Oh, please. You're an expert," she countered, taking another sip of her latte. "And with that accent of yours, it's a double threat."

"The accent can't be helped, though I'll try to tone down my charm if I'm so irresistible to you."

"I didn't say that."

She didn't have to, his skin was all but buzzing still from what they'd shared the night before. He knew her body. Knew her mind. And knew she was trying to cover her physical reactions to him.

"Ah, that's lovely. We've no problems then, have we?" Point scored, he lifted his coffee cup and eased carefully against the back of the seat, half expecting it to break off and send him to the tile floor in a sprawl.

"No problem at all." Reaching for her purse, Laura pulled out a small tablet and a pen, then looked at him. "So, what kind of house do you have in mind?"

He shrugged and took a sip of his latte. "I'll know it when I see it."

"That's not much help in the looking department." She tapped her pen against her pad in a show of nerves. How like Laura, the old-fashioned girl, to prefer paper and pen to a computer tablet. He found it almost endearing.

Then, as that thought settled in, he scowled a little and reminded himself just who was in charge of this game between them.

"Well," he said, "we've known each other some time, so what kind of house do you see me in?"

Laura tipped her head to one side, studied him thoughtfully for a moment and started with "Big, for one."

He laughed and shifted unsteadily on the tiny café chair. "Aye, that's a good start."

"Near or on the water," she continued.

"I do love the sea. Comes from growing up so near to it, I suppose."

It was something they'd had in common when first they'd met, he thought. Her, born and raised in a California beach town and he on the other side of the world, had found common ground in their love of the ocean. The Pacific was too mild and tame for Ronan's taste though. He preferred the Atlantic where the waves raged and thundered against Ireland's shores.

And then there was Lough Mask, he thought, near his home, as wide and beautiful as the sea, but with a calmness that soothed. A pang of something echoed inside him and Ronan realized he was homesick. He'd been gone from Ireland for nearly six months and his soul yearned for it.

She nodded, made another note on her pad and said, "You love books, so a library would be good. And either a separate office or a library big enough to serve as both."

Ronan smiled. She did know him well. And what did that mean? He'd never spent enough time with any one woman for her to know him as well as Laura apparently did. Ronan scowled to himself as one simple fact reached up and grabbed him at the base of his throat.

He was in deeper with Laura than he had thought.

Yet he couldn't make himself back away. He wanted her. His body ached for her right now, so letting her go was out of the question.

"You can't cook," she said, interrupting his train of thought, "so I'm guessing a kitchen a housekeeper or chef would love…"

He had to laugh. "I only burned the soup that once," he insisted. "And you were distracting me at the time."

He could still see her in memory, perched naked on the granite counter at the Laguna house, smiling at him. Welcoming him as he forgot all about the soup on the stove and gathered her close. Their lovemaking had been fast and hard and completely satisfying—until they had heard the hiss of the soup boiling over.

"It was canned soup, Ronan," she said, "and you managed to ruin it."

"As I recall, 'twas worth it," he mused and enjoyed seeing the flash of memory dart across her eyes leaving behind a smudge of desire.

"Yeah, well," Laura said, dropping her gaze to the

pad in front of her. "Moving on. You like a lot of privacy, too, so you won't want a close neighbor."

"True enough." He shuddered at the thought. His home in Ireland was a manor house with its own damn park surrounding it. His closest neighbor, Maeve Carroll, lived in a cottage almost half a mile from him and the village was beyond that. "Don't know how you accept people being able to peer over fences at you. See into your tiny yards, into your lives whenever they're of a mind."

"It's called being neighborly."

"Or annoying."

"You know," she said, shaking her head, "just because you *can* spy on your neighbor doesn't mean you *do* it."

He shook his head. "You mean I'm to trust my fellow man? I don't think so."

"Trust runs both ways, Ronan," she said, then cleared her throat and continued before he could comment. "Several bedrooms, I think, in case you have…guests." She bent her head to make a note and Ronan fisted his hands to keep from reaching out to touch the sunlit fall of her hair.

Grumbling under his breath at his own ragged control, he tried to get back on topic. "That's a good point. I'll have people coming in from Cosain, Galway from time to time…"

"So," she interrupted, "basically, you want a mansion all by itself on the ocean with plenty of room for books and guests."

"Sounds perfect."

She frowned. "And not easy to find."

"Then we'd best get looking, hadn't we?" He stood up and instinctively held her chair for her to rise and stand beside him. When she had, he touched her face and with his fingertips, turned it up to him.

"Trust is something that comes hard to me," he said quietly.

"I know." She moved her head enough to have his fingers slide from her skin.

"Aye, I suppose so as you *do* know a bit about me, Laura," he said, keeping his voice low, for her ears only. "But there's more yet to learn."

Around them, Carmen's bakery was a hive of conversation, laughter and the bright buzz of people enjoying their morning. But here, in this corner, there was just the two of them.

Ronan looked into clear blue eyes, and saw only wariness looking back at him. A part of him regretted that. A larger part wondered how long it would take him to turn that suspicion into passion again.

Seven

For two weeks, they spent every day together. And every day, Ronan chipped away at Laura's resolve.

It wasn't outright. Nothing she could call him on, nothing that would allow her to warn him to back off. No, he was sneakier than that.

He held her chair for her at lunch and would let his fingertips trail across her shoulders as she seated herself. He put his hand at the small of her back when they climbed stairs to some of the cliff-side homes she showed him. She felt his touch all the way to her bones and she *knew* he was well aware of what he was doing.

When she spoke, he gave her his full attention, his gaze locked with hers as if she were the most important being on earth. The heat in his gaze was unmistakable and impossible to ignore. He knew that, too. She was sure of it.

And for two weeks, he found something wrong with

every property she showed him. Too small. Too big. Too high on the cliff, too low on the hillside. Not near enough to the ocean, too close to the crash of waves. He was perfectly reasonable about it, but the upshot was the same. He was dragging out their time together and Laura was on the ragged edge of her control.

It was all well and good to make a vow of chastity where Ronan was concerned—but keeping that vow was turning out to be even more difficult than she had thought it would be.

Especially, she thought, when he spent more time at her house than he did at his. Even now, he was sprawled companionably on the couch beside her, long legs stretched out, feet crossed at the ankles. When he stirred, it was to grab another slice of pizza from the open box on the coffee table in front of them.

He broke off a piece of crust before tossing it to Beast. Then, taking a sip of his beer, he looked at her and winked. "You're watching me in the way a woman does when she's thinking something."

"I'm thinking you look awfully comfortable."

"And why shouldn't I? It's a lovely house, there's a fire in the hearth, a lovely woman at my side and a dog at me feet."

"Thank you very much," Georgia said from the chair.

"I beg your pardon," Ronan corrected himself with a blinding grin. "*Two* lovely women."

"Much better." Georgia lifted her wineglass in a silent toast.

"You're no help," Laura told her sister.

"Was I supposed to help?" Georgia hid her grin behind her wineglass as she took another sip.

"So, you don't want me to be comfortable?" Ronan asked.

"I just don't understand why you have to be comfortable *here*."

"Because, love, you have yet to find me a suitable house to buy."

"You could go to the one you *rent*."

"Did you hear that, Georgia?" Ronan shook his head sadly and lowered his voice dramatically. "She wants me away to sit by myself in that empty house rather than be here with *friends*." As he said that last word, he turned his gaze on Laura meaningfully.

She knew what he was doing, but damned if she could find a way to stop him. If she tried to bar him from the house, Georgia would only let him in anyway.

"Beast is getting fat," Ronan mused as he picked up the wine bottle and refilled Laura's and Georgia's glasses.

"Then stop sneaking him pizza," Laura told him.

"Ah," Ronan countered. "But he *wants* it so."

"Sometimes what we want isn't good for us," she argued.

"And sometimes the wanting is all we have, and we should enjoy it for what it is."

"And sometimes," Georgia said, "other people in the room get tired of hearing people speak in code."

Laura grumbled, but otherwise kept quiet as Georgia flicked on the TV and a cable news program came on. Georgia was a news addict, and Laura couldn't understand it. From what she could tell, it was mostly bad news anyway.

"Where is this house you want to show me tomorrow?" Ronan asked and Laura turned her head to look at him.

Lamplight glowed softly behind him. To one side was the fireplace, flames snapping and hissing as they devoured the wood. Laura held out one of the two property sheets she held in her hand toward Ronan and waited for him to take it.

"There are two, actually," she said, pleased to be back on solid ground, even though she knew darn well that he would dismiss whatever palatial estate she showed him. Even the lovely one that he barely glanced at before handing back to her. "That one is in Dana Point, farther south along the coast. The house was built only three years ago. It's a Cape Cod style, but—"

"It won't do." Ronan eased closer to her on the couch.

"You didn't even look at the picture, Ronan," she said. "You could at least wait to see the house before saying no."

"There'd be no point. I've no interest in a Cape Cod style. Lovely as they are, they don't speak to me."

"Well, what *does* speak to you, for heaven's sake?"

"You do," he murmured.

Something inside her fluttered excitedly into life. Laura squashed that little bud of hope like a bug. Flirting came so easily to him, it was second nature. Desire was just as easy and meant as little. Without real feelings behind the passion, what was the point?

She'd learned that lesson and didn't intend to forget it. "Don't go there."

"Why the bloody hell not?" he whispered, lowering his voice so that Georgia wouldn't hear, as focused as she was on the television across the room. "We're good together."

"In bed," she qualified.

"Exactly," he agreed cheerfully.

Why was he working so hard to get her back into bed? There were women all over the world who would fall across his sheets with a whoop of glee if he so much as glanced at them. That thought burned a little.

"You're making this seem more difficult than it is," he said.

"No," she qualified, dismissing the mental image of women lining up for a crack at the gorgeous Irishman. Because really, she couldn't do anything about that. Once he realized that they really were over, he'd move on and find someone more willing than she. And Laura wouldn't have a thing to say about it.

"I'm not the one being difficult. You are. I've already told you—"

He cut her off neatly. "Why don't we talk about this alone?" He nodded toward Georgia. "We could go outside, take a walk."

Oh, sure, alone with him in the dark. That would be a good call.

"It's cold outside," Laura pointed out, settling more deeply into the sofa cushions.

"I can keep you warm," he offered, then grinned. "Not in a romantic way, mind you. Just in the way of being friendly…"

"Uh-huh. No. Thanks." She nodded to where her sister sat engrossed in the evening news. "I don't want to abandon Georgia."

"Or is it more that you don't trust yourself alone with me?"

She laughed, though that little lie was harder to pull off than she might have imagined. Heck, yes, she didn't trust herself. Ronan was hard to ignore when he *wasn't* trying. When he was actually working at seducing a woman, he was damn near irresistible.

Still, he didn't need to know that. "Oh, I think I can keep from flinging myself into your manly arms."

"Don't bother on my account."

"Ronan, we had a deal," she reminded him. "No flirting."

"This isn't flirting, this is just chatting."

"Then no chatting, either."

"You're a hard woman."

"You betcha," she said and felt about as hard as a marshmallow. Yeah, she was tough. That's why she took cold showers every night and then fell into a dream-filled sleep. Dreams in which she wasn't nearly so disciplined, instead giving in to exactly what she wanted. And every morning, she woke up exhausted, her body strung with tension only to face a day spent saying no to Ronan.

If she ever did manage to sell him a house, she would have seriously earned that commission.

"If you'd listen to reason…" he said.

"I'm not the one being unreasonable…" she countered.

"If you guys are going to do battle, could you do it in the kitchen?" Georgia asked, never taking her gaze from the news channel.

"No battle here, only clashing opinions," Ronan said.

"Do you want mine?" Georgia asked.

"No," Laura spoke up fast. She already knew her sister's opinion. Hadn't she heard it every day for the past two weeks?

Use him and lose him seemed to be the main theme. Which was easy enough to understand since Georgia was still a little bitter about her ex-husband. But Laura already knew that option wasn't for her. She'd tried to lose him and look what had happened. He had plopped himself into her world and showed no signs of leaving.

Using him though, was way too tempting.

His cell phone rang. Ronan checked the readout and stood up. "I've a need to take this, sorry."

Laura shrugged, but wondered who was calling. One of the millions of women already making her move? She watched him go, headed for the kitchen and some privacy. Her gaze fixed on his butt, and she sighed a little at the view.

"Oh, yeah." Georgia muffled a laugh. "You don't want him. That's so clear."

"I love you," Laura said. "Now, shut up."

"I just don't get why you have to torture yourself. What does it prove? That you're tough? Well congrats. We all know how strong you are."

"This isn't about being strong"

"Then what is it about?"

"Being *safe,*" she said before she could think about it. When the words were out, she realized that was the simple truth. She'd allowed Ronan to mean too much to her. Allowed fantasies and dreams to replace reality. She'd set herself up to be disappointed. Hurt. Ronan had walked away because he didn't want what she wanted. Well, nothing had changed, had it? They were still light-years apart on that score. Why go back for more pain?

"Safe is overrated," Georgia said, watching her.

"Says the woman who hasn't had a date in six months."

"I'm picky."

"You're scared."

Georgia scowled at her. "I've got reasons."

"So do I," Laura said, "so let's leave it at that."

Georgia hit the mute button on the TV and turned around in her chair so she could face Laura. "You know I love you, right? But you're nuts."

"What?" She shot a look at the kitchen doorway, making sure Ronan was out of earshot.

"Are you going for sainthood here, or are you just trying to kill Ronan?"

"Neither, thanks. Don't you have a news program to watch?"

"Please, like I'm really watching it." Georgia shook her head. "Since you won't split up our happy little threesome, I was *trying* to give you some privacy. Maybe I should just go upstairs."

"Don't." Laura frowned at her sister. "If you do, I swear I'll never make you another chocolate cake as long as you live."

Grimacing, Georgia admitted, "You fight dirty, but okay. My point is, he wants you. You want him. Why the hell not?"

"You know why not."

"Honey, I feel for you." Georgia's voice softened and dropped into a deeper whisper. "I know what losing the baby did to you. How it hurt you when Ronan left. But in case you haven't noticed...*he's back*."

"For how long?"

"Who knows? Isn't that the point?" Georgia tucked her short blond hair behind her ears and reminded her sister, "Even when you think it's forever—that doesn't mean it will be."

A twinge of guilt had Laura wincing a little. She knew how her sister had loved that moron who had vowed 'until death do us part' and then left her for a brainless cheerleader.

"I can't do temporary, Georgia. I just can't."

"We *all* do temporary, sweetie. It's just that most of us don't know it until it's too late."

Ronan walked back into the room and looked from

Laura to Georgia and back again. "Did I miss something?"

"No," Georgia said before Laura could. "Just some sister stuff."

"Everything okay?" Laura asked.

"Yes, and no," he said. "There's some trouble at home I've to see to. I'll be flying home to Ireland in the morning."

She didn't even look surprised, Ronan thought, and that irritated him. Well, he'd no interest in leaving just yet, either, but he couldn't ignore the phone call, could he? Clearly, Laura had just been waiting for him to leave again. And now he was accommodating her. Another irritation.

Followed by inspiration.

"Come with me."

"What?" Laura laughed and shook her head. "Go with you? To Ireland?"

"Aye, to Ireland." It was perfect, he told himself. He'd been trying to get her back into his bed for weeks now and having her in Ireland—with nowhere to run—could only help him in his quest. She was completely off guard now, and he intended to keep her that way.

"You're serious."

"Absolutely. Do you have a passport?"

"Well, sure, but—"

"Then there's no problem."

"There's a huge problem. I can't just go running off to another country. I've got a business and…a *dog*…"

Beast thumped his tail.

"Are you trying to say that Georgia's incapable of running your business for a week or two?"

"Two?"

"I've business to see to at home and while I'm there, I

should check in at the offices in Galway as well," Ronan told her truthfully. "It's been six months and though phone calls serve well, it's no substitute for the boss actually being there."

"Oh, sure," Laura said, standing up and moving away from him. "Check in at work."

"I'll show you my country as you've shown me yours." He kept his voice low, tempting, and smiled inwardly as he watched her waver.

"This is ridiculous," she said, though her voice was a little less decisive than it had been a moment or two ago. "I can't—"

She looked at Georgia and the two women exchanged some sort of silent communication that he couldn't interpret. But Ronan had the feeling he was about to lose, which he wouldn't allow to happen.

He wanted her all to himself, he thought. And having the home ground advantage wouldn't hurt his case, either. He'd get her out of her safety zone and into his and see what happened between them then.

And more than that, Ronan realized, he just wanted her with him. He didn't care to explore the reasons why. So he made her an offer he knew she would find hard to refuse.

"Go with me, Laura, and I'll buy the place you showed me yesterday."

Her jaw dropped. "You'll—"

For the first time, Georgia spoke up. "Which house?"

"The Barret estate," Laura said, her gaze locked with Ronan's even as she answered her sister.

"Are you kidding?" Georgia pushed herself to her feet and went to her sister, sending one curious glance at Ronan as if she couldn't believe what he was saying.

But he meant every word. He needed a place, and

he'd only been dragging out the looking for the chance to have Laura to himself. If he got her on his plane, that part of the puzzle was solved. Besides, the estate wasn't far from the home he was renting now. Though it was bigger, closer to the ocean and boasted a lot of acreage for such a small beach town.

In fact, the place was damn near perfect. He just hadn't wanted to buy it and end this time with Laura. Now though, he could use that purchase to his own advantage—the only way Ronan liked to conclude a deal.

"The Barret estate's been for sale for a year and a half," Georgia said.

"I know." Laura looked at her sister, then to Ronan. He could see the wheels in her brain turning. Considering.

"The commission on that house would be—"

"I *know*," Laura said. "It would be enough for us to buy our building."

"Boy howdy," Georgia whispered, slanting a look at Ronan. "You're *good*."

He gave her a nod. "Thank you."

"This is blackmail," Laura said.

He smiled. "What's your point?"

Georgia snorted and Laura gave her a dark look.

"You realize that if I do this, you'll have to handle the business on your own for a week."

"Or two," Ronan put in.

"Or *two*," she corrected.

"Yeah, that'll be rough. In case you haven't noticed? Business is not booming," Georgia reminded her, and Ronan knew that was another weight on his side.

If it were just for herself, Laura might tell him no just on principle. But he also knew her well enough to know that she would do this for Georgia. Because it was important to her to do what she could to protect her family. He could admire that even while using it to get what he wanted.

"You bring the sale papers with you and once we're in Ireland, I'll sign them." His gaze locked with hers, and he waited, letting her think. Letting her worry it all out in her mind, though they both knew she would agree in the end.

"She'll do it," Georgia said flatly.

"Hey!" Laura turned on her.

Ignoring Ronan, Georgia looked at her sister and said, "Please. Don't be an idiot about this. I'll take care of Beast and work and you'll take a vacation and come back with enough money to buy our building for us. It's a no-brainer, Laura. For God's sake, don't be stubborn about this."

"Thanks for the support," she said wryly.

"Oh, I'm supportive," Georgia told her, then shot a look at Ronan. "But I'm not stupid, either. He's got his reasons for inviting you—"

"Hey now," Ronan blurted.

"—and you've got reasons to accept. It's like a devil's bargain only everybody wins."

"Bargains with a devil?" Laura asked, turning her gaze to Ronan. "Does that ever work out well?"

Ronan walked to her and held out one hand to seal their deal. "Try me and see."

He had her; he knew he had her. He felt it in his bones. So why then, he wondered, did he not relax until she slid her much smaller hand into his and say, "Okay, devil. You win this round."

He intended to win them all.

* * *

Laura was used to living on the periphery of the rich and famous. She dealt with wealthy clients all the time, yet she'd never actually been treated as though she belonged.

Until today.

Flying on a luxurious, private jet, being waited on by a flight attendant, drinking champagne at lunch. Taking a whirlwind trip through New York City in the back of a limo while the jet was being refueled.

She felt like a princess.

And Ronan, darn it, was the perfect Prince Charming.

Every time he looked at her, Laura's heart ached a little because it was all so wonderful and so doomed. Nothing had changed. This spur-of-the-moment trip wouldn't lead to happily-ever-after, and she knew it. It was blackmail, plain and simple. He'd dangled financial freedom in front of her, knowing that she couldn't turn it down—not just for herself, but for her sister.

Still high in the sky, with the jewel of Ireland beneath them, shining a brilliant green against the deep blue of the ocean, Ronan looked at her. As if he knew what she was thinking, he asked, "Do you have the papers ready then?"

"I do," she told him, and reached into her purse. Pulling out the folded sale agreement, she handed it to him and watched as he gave it one final look.

He'd already read the contract from front to back during the first hour of their flight, so it didn't take him long to flip through to the back page and sign his name with a flourish.

When he gave the contract back, Laura smiled. No

matter what happened now, she and Georgia would be able to buy their building. Grow their business.

"You can fax the contract to Georgia from my home office," he said. "Then it'll be official."

"Okay, I will." She folded it back up, tucked the contract away in her purse and told herself she wouldn't give it another thought.

The promise of financial security might have gotten her here, but now that she *was* here, she was going to take Georgia's advice. As the jet prepared to land, she looked at Ronan and smiled. He gave her a wink and she remembered exactly what her sister had said just before Laura left for the airport.

"You'll have two weeks with him, sweetie. And in two weeks, you can either get him out of your heart altogether—or you can let him back in." Georgia gave her a hard hug and a kiss on the cheek. *"Either way, this is the trip of a lifetime, so try to enjoy it."*

Laura intended to.

"Welcome to Ireland." Ronan's whisper sounded in her ear as Laura stepped off the sleek, private jet and was met by a cold blast of wind that slapped color into her cheeks and stole her breath.

She stood at the top of the stairs—she knew there was another word for them, she just couldn't think of it—and looked out around her. They were in a small, regional airport somewhere in County Mayo, according to Ronan. Here there was no huge terminal. There was just an open tarmac, surrounded by fields so green, it almost hurt to look at them. The artist in her itched to find a paintbrush and attempt to capture what she saw.

A smile curved her mouth as she whipped her head from side to side, trying to take everything in at once. She might still be furious at how he'd blackmailed her into the trip, but she wasn't foolish enough to let her anger spoil her first trip to Europe.

Although, the first thing she realized was, she shouldn't have worn a dress and heels. She was already cold. But flying on a private jet had seemed to require a bit dressier appearance than her normal slacks and shirt.

"Cold?"

"A little," she said, grateful at least that her dark green dress had long sleeves even if the scooped neck left too much of her chest exposed to the wind. Her black heels wobbled slightly on the metal stairs, but that might have been nerves.

Ronan took her hand in his and the heat that jumped from his body to hers eased the chill of the Irish wind, but only stirred the flutters in her stomach into double-time. He was dangerous to her and no matter what happened on this trip, she'd better keep that in mind.

He led her down the steps and walked beside her to the waiting car.

"I hope you're not too tired. It's an hour or so to the village and my home," he was saying as she walked to the passenger side, him right behind her.

"I'm not tired at all," she admitted, flashing him a wide smile in spite of her trepidation. "I'm in *Ireland*."

He chuckled, then put one hand on her arm. "Did you want to drive us then?" he asked, a smile in his voice.

"What? No."

"Then perhaps you should go to the other side."

Laura looked down and realized that she was standing at what should have been the passenger door. Of course over here, the steering wheel was on the right.

"Oh, okay. Weird."

"'Tis only weird to you. To me, it's the proper way of doing things."

While their luggage was piled into the back of the Rover, Laura took her seat and buckled in. Ronan then fired up the engine and headed out.

"We're headed for the village of Dunley and my home beyond."

"Didn't you say Cosain was headquartered in Galway?"

"It is," he said, steering the car down a road that seemed to shrink in width the farther they drove along it. "But my home is in Dunley."

She turned her head to stare out the window at the passing scenery. "I've never seen so many different shades of green. It's so beautiful. Everywhere I look, it's a picture. A painting waiting to happen. I wish I'd thought to bring my paints with me."

"We can pick up some paints and things for you in Westport. It's not far from the village."

She shot him a quick look over her shoulder, trying to read the expression in his eyes. Was he just being nice, or was there some other motive behind his offer? Hard to tell, so she'd just accept it for what it was. "I'd love that."

Green fields, crisscrossed by stone walls and dotted with black and white sheep spread out on either side of the car. In the distance, a smudge of purple on the horizon heralded the mountains. The sky was gray, the wind tearing across the fields. There were ruins, too. Crumbling stone towers that told stories of chivalry and greatness centuries ago.

"So many," Laura mused, voice soft. "Castles and towers and they're all still here."

"Aye," he said, glancing at the nearest crumbling spire of stone. "Their battles are done, their stone walls chipping away, but the echoes linger. They remind us. Always."

"Remind you of what?"

He shot her another fast look. "That the Irish fight for what we hold dear. What we want, we get."

There was a rumble of warning in his voice and she shivered at the sound of it. "And what if they don't want it anymore once they've got it?"

"Well then, that would be a whole different problem, wouldn't it?"

A few minutes later, they were parked in the road, waiting while a woman herded a cow toward home.

"You have interesting traffic jams," Laura said, laughing.

"Aye," he agreed. "And there's no point in honking. It would be considered rude and the cow wouldn't care at any rate."

"It's great. And it explains why you're so patient with the traffic in California."

"Ah, you don't know traffic until you've waited for an entire herd of sheep to make their way along the road."

"You're happy to be home," she said, watching him.

"I am at that." He looked away from her, to stare out over the fields and Laura watched his features soften. "Every time I come home, I can't imagine why I ever left."

"You know, I watched the way people hustled around all day, leaping to do your bidding."

"My bidding?" he countered with a short laugh. "You make me sound like a tyrant."

"Not a tyrant," she corrected. "Maybe a king."

"Ah, King Ronan," he mused. "I like that."

"I'm not surprised," she said. "But my point is, on

the plane, in New York, you were distant. More formal. But now you're—"

He turned his head to look at her and in the soft morning light, his features were shadowed, his blue eyes burning with intensity. "I'm what?"

"Different." Since landing in Ireland, it was as if Ronan's heart had opened up. She saw it in his eyes, on his features as he looked around at the country he loved. He was more…*real,* than she'd ever seen him. And that made him more dangerous to her heart than ever.

She'd convinced herself to enjoy this trip and then let go of the controlling, bossy, arrogant businessman Ronan Connolly, despite how it hurt to let go of the dream.

But this Ronan…Laura didn't know if she'd be able to let him go when the time came.

"What do you think of my island then, Laura Page?"

"So far," she admitted, when he gave her a quick look, "I love it."

"Good answer," he said, smiling. "A very good answer."

A few miles further on, he turned off the road into a wide gravel drive lined by chrysanthemums, their bright colors looking bedraggled by wind and rain.

The lovely house at the end of the wide, gravel drive was gray stone, two stories tall and spread out from the middle into two wide wings. Windowpanes glittered in the early morning sun.

"Home," Ronan told her and shut off the engine.

Stunned, Laura climbed out of the car to stand on the graveled drive. Her gaze swept over the manor house, the grounds around it and finally, to him, only to find Ronan watching her.

"Okay, now I understand why you didn't like any of

the houses I showed you." She looked back at the house that had no doubt stood for centuries. "If you were comparing them to this one, there's just no contest."

"Oh," he said, "there's one house at the beach that has something this one doesn't."

"Really?" She shifted her gaze back to him. "Which one?"

"The one where you live, Laura."

She pulled in a long deep breath and let it out slowly, hoping to steady herself. But who was she fooling? There was no balance around Ronan. Ever. And being on his home turf now, she knew she was asking for trouble. Yet, she couldn't seem to care.

The front door was painted a bright cherry-red and when it flew open a deep *woof* shattered the quiet. A huge, black-and-white English sheepdog bolted from the house and *flew* across the drive, headed right at Ronan.

"Deirdre!" He laughed, braced himself and only rocked in place when the giant dog slammed into him. His big hands scrubbed at her fur, scratched behind her ears, sending the dog into spasms of ecstasy.

Crouching beside her, Ronan looked up at Laura and said, "Meet Deirdre, named for one of Ireland's mythic heroes."

Before Laura could speak, the dog was up and scuttling for her, prepared to pounce in exuberant greeting.

"No!" Ronan shouted and Deirdre dropped to her butt and wiggled in place.

Charmed and delighted at the wildly excitable dog that had thankfully broken the tension between she and Ronan, Laura bent down, and swiped the dog's hair back from its eyes. Deirdre swiped her tongue across Laura's face as welcome.

"An Irishman with an *English* sheepdog?" Laura

asked, still laughing as she wiped her face and looked up at the man who'd come to stand beside her.

"I'm not so small a man I can't admit that the Brits do *some* things right. And they did with Deirdre's breed."

He took her hand and she felt that now-familiar zing of something wicked sweep through her body. As if he knew exactly what she was feeling, he squeezed her hand, winked at her and said, "Come along then, see my home."

Said the spider to the fly.

Eight

As webs went, it was a beauty, was all Laura could think.

Deirdre raced ahead of them, her claws clattering on the gleaming oak floorboards and sliding every time she hit one of the colorful rugs scattered about.

The walls were painted a soft blue and dotted with paintings—family portraits, mainly. While Ronan strode through the house, searching for who, she didn't know, Laura took a moment to study the faces glaring down at her.

One man in particular looked as if he wanted to chew his way through the painting and clamber back into the world to rule it. The woman at his side, though lovely, looked no happier to be trapped in her canvas.

"My parents," Ronan told her, coming up behind her so quietly she hadn't heard his approach. Startled, and feeling a little guilty for what she'd been thinking, she

turned to look at him. She could see the resemblance,
she noted, though she'd never seen real coldness in his
expression. Until now.

"Where are they now?"

He shrugged as if her question meant little to him.
"Sniping at each other, no doubt, caught between Heaven
and Hell as neither of them can agree on a thing."

"Oh, I'm sorry."

"'Twas a long time ago," he said, his gaze shifting
from her to the portrait and back again. "They died in
a car accident, the two of them, more than ten years
back now."

She thought of her own parents, happily nesting in
Oregon, and how she would feel if she lost them. "It
must have been hard to lose them both so suddenly."

Ronan's gaze caught hers. "Don't put emotions where
you think they should be," he said. "My parents were
as unhappy a pair as you'd ever meet and made sure to
share that feeling with their only son."

"Ronan—"

He shook his head and took her hand, leading her
into the front room. "I found Patsy, my housekeeper,
in the kitchen. She's made tea and will be bringing it
to the parlor right along."

"Okay." He didn't want to talk about his parents so
they wouldn't. But Laura had to admit, at least privately,
that learning about his parents helped her to understand
him a bit better. No wonder he didn't make much of family. Or love. No wonder he hadn't known how to react
when she'd told him of their lost baby.

Her mind still working on the problem of Ronan, she
stopped dead and smiled as she looked at the room. The
parlor was amazing. A white-tiled hearth, where a fire
burned cheerfully against the gloom of the day. Pale

green walls hung with seascapes. Oversize couches facing each other across a wide table that held a Waterford crystal bowl of autumn flowers.

"It's lovely."

"Aye, it is," he said, stalking across the room to a spindle table that held a selection of crystal decanters. He picked up a tumbler, poured himself a drink, then turned to look at her, one hand resting on the mantel.

Laura sank onto one of the couches, her knees gone suddenly weak. God, he was gorgeous. In America, he had swept her right off her feet without effort. Here, in his home, he was even more devastating. He belonged here. Lord of the Manor, she thought, catching the glint of pride in his eyes. And at once, her mind turned to the ruined towers and castles they'd seen on their trip here. He could have stepped out of the past, she thought. Irish warrior. Proud. Strong. Unrelenting.

A chill swept across her skin and she shivered.

"Cold still?" he asked.

"No, I'm good." Just crazy, she thought, to even be entertaining the kind of thoughts racing through her mind at the moment. She wanted him so badly, she ached with it. But sleeping with him would change nothing. He was still not the man for her. And if she let herself feel more for him, wouldn't the pain be that much sharper when it inevitably ended?

"Ah, here's tea."

Patsy Brennan was short, with graying black hair scraped into a bun at the back of her neck. Her pale skin was milk smooth and her blue eyes held traces of tears. "Here we go, then. Hello, miss. Welcome to Ireland."

"Thank you," Laura said as the woman set a tray down in front of her on the table. There was a plate of sandwiches, another plate holding freshly iced, tiny cakes and a teapot with violets running its circumference. "It looks wonderful."

"Kind of you to say. Now I'll just be off to—"

"What's wrong, Patsy?" Ronan asked.

"Nothing a'tall," the woman assured him. "And it's nothing for the now, anyway."

Laura kept her head down and poured herself a cup of tea.

"If it's not for now, then there is something," Ronan told her. "And your own Sinead called me only yesterday to tell me there was trouble, so what's it about then?"

"She shouldn't have called." Patsy straightened up, all five feet of her, and gathered such a look of dignity about her, she could have been a queen.

"Aye, well, she did. And why shouldn't she call?" Ronan asked, walking toward the older woman. "She's been like a sister to me all these years and you more a mother than I ever knew."

Patsy frowned at him. "You had a fine mother and all and this isn't the time."

Laura sank back into the couch cushions, trying to be invisible. If she'd had the slightest idea where to go from this room, she might have bolted. Instead, she was caught.

"Laura's a...*friend*," Ronan said and she scowled into her tea. A friend. A friend who had shared his bed, lost his child and had been blackmailed into a trip to Ireland that was getting more interesting by the minute. "You can say what you will in front of her."

Frowning still, Patsy folded her arms beneath her comfortable bosom and tapped the toe of one shoe against the flowered rug beneath her feet. Throwing an apologetic glance at Laura, she said, "I'll beg your pardon for his manners. It seems his rearing was somewhat lacking."

"It's okay," Laura said, waving off the apology and picking up a cake.

"You've no need to apologize for me," Ronan said. "Now tell me what the trouble is so I can fix it and be done."

"As pushy a man as you were a child," she said, half to herself and had Laura snorting in agreement. "Always did think you knew the way of things and that everyone else should simply say, 'Aye, Ronan,' and go along."

"Hmm…" Laura said.

"Oh, miss," Patsy told her with a sharp nod, "I could tell you stories about himself and his cousin Sean…"

"Please, call me Laura." She took a bite of the cake and nearly groaned with pleasure.

"I will then and thank you, Laura. You're a patient woman to be putting up with—"

Ronan's shout caught both their attentions. "Will you tell me the bloody trouble?"

"There's no trouble," came a male voice from the doorway.

They all turned to see Sean Connolly, standing in between a young couple. Sean's dark brown hair was wind-ruffled and his long-sleeved white shirt had grass stains on it. He looked rumpled, but proud.

The girl beside him had short black hair, tear-stained blue eyes that were too much like Patsy's for the girl to be anyone but her daughter Sinead. And the boy had what promised to be an impressive black eye blooming on his face.

"Sean, what're you doing here?" Ronan demanded, shifting his gaze from his cousin to the couple to Patsy.

"Will somebody please tell me what the bloody hell is going on?"

"Laura," Sean said, a wide grin splitting his face, "'tis good to see you again!"

"Thanks." She hadn't seen Sean since the night he had dropped Beast off at her house what felt like years ago. "You look busy."

"Aye, I have been," he admitted, then gave the boy in his grip a hard look. "But 'tis settled now."

"He hit Michael," Sinead cried, jerking a thumb at Sean.

"I did and will again," Sean agreed.

The boy, Michael, Laura guessed, tried to make a break for it, but Sean tightened his hold on him before he could take a step. "Easy on, boy'o. You're not going anywhere."

"Ronan," Sinead complained, "tell Sean to let him go."

"Not until I know what's going on in my own damned house!" Ronan's shout was even louder this time, and Laura winced. She was pretty sure she heard the window glass rattle in the panes.

"Language!" Patsy snapped.

Ronan swiped one hand across his face, Sean shook Michael like a dog with a bone, Sinead wailed piteously and Laura fervently wished that she was holding a martini instead of a cup of tea.

"There's to be a wedding," Sean told him then leaned into the captive boy. "Isn't there, young Michael O'Connor?"

The kid nodded.

Laura felt for him even though she hadn't a clue what was going on.

"I'll not marry him!" Sinead lifted her chin and

stalked to the window seat across the room. She dropped onto it with all of the drama a young woman could muster and stared off through the panes at the gray day beyond.

Ronan looked at his cousin. "Why should she marry him?"

"She's carrying his baby, and he's decided to do the right thing, haven't you, Michael?"

"Aye," Michael muttered.

"Baby?" Ronan echoed.

"A wedding?" Laura said.

"More tea, miss?" Patsy asked.

Ronan felt as if his head might explode.

And at the moment, he would have welcomed it.

Patsy shouted at Sinead, Sinead shouted at Sean, Sean shouted at Michael, and Ronan shouted at all of them. The only sensible person in the room was Laura. And she sat on the sofa, watching them all as if they were on the bloody television.

"I'll not marry a man you had to chase down like a dog," Sinead told Sean.

"I didn't run," Michael said.

"Oh, aye, a fast walk, then?" Sean sneered at the boy.

Sinead pregnant? How was that possible, he asked himself. Only a day or so ago, she was twelve, playing with dolls in the garden. Following him about like a puppy, peppering him with questions. His heart turned over in his chest. Somehow he had missed her growing up on him.

Pregnant.

Was there an epidemic he hadn't heard about? His friend Sam Travis's wife was having a child. Now Sinead. And of course, he thought, his gaze sliding to the woman sipping tea as casually as if she were alone in the room, there was Laura.

She'd had his child inside her. A stir of something he couldn't identify rushed through him. Would she have been any easier to talk to than Sinead had Laura kept the baby? Would he have faced her down in a shouting match over a marriage he would have insisted on?

Laura looked up just then and caught him looking at her. In her eyes, he saw shadows, and he knew that she, too, was thinking of their own situation and comparing it, now, to Sinead's. They would have to talk about this. But for the moment, there were the loud shouts in the room to deal with.

"Sinead," Ronan bellowed, and got everyone's attention. "Let's make this as simple as possible. Are you carrying Michael's child?"

She sniffed, wiped away a single angry tear and lifted her chin. "I am."

"Then you'll marry," he said flatly, sparing one warning glare at the father of the girl's baby. "As soon as we can manage."

"As it should be," Sean said, satisfied.

"The banns could be read at Mass as early as Sunday," Patsy was saying, more to herself than anyone else.

"I told her I'd marry her already. You didn't have to blacken my eye," Michael said.

"'Twas fun," Sean assured him.

Sinead hopped up from the window seat, rushed across the room and slapped both hands against Ronan's chest in accusation.

"I called you to *help* me," she said, hurt in her voice and shining in her eyes.

"I am, lass." Ronan looked at her with sympathy. "Why don't you want to marry him?"

"Because I'll be no man's *duty,*" she said with a glare over her shoulder for the boy who was her lover. "I'll marry for love or I won't marry at all."

"Love?" Ronan took her shoulders in his big hands and held her still when she might have skittered to one side. He looked into her face and saw her as a child and now as the woman she was and his heart turned over. He could sympathize with what she was feeling, but he knew what was best for her. "Did you love him when you made the child?"

She looked down, to the side, above her head, anywhere but into his gaze. But Ronan waited her out and hardly noticed the hush in the room. Finally, she looked up at him and whispered, "Yes."

"And did he love you?"

"I did, and I do," Michael called out from where Sean still kept a wary hand on his shoulder.

Ronan ignored the boy and focused on Sinead. "You'll marry, Sinead. You've wanted Michael since you were sixteen and nothing's changed. Only the timing of the thing."

"I don't want him to *have* to marry me," she insisted.

"Responsibility's never an easy thing, but it's the only way and well you know it," Patsy put in from where she sat on the couch.

Ronan took a quick look at Laura who was biting her bottom lip as if forcing herself to be quiet.

"Responsibility shouldn't be the reason for a proposal," Sinead argued, turning from Ronan to face her mother.

"It's not like that, Sinead," Michael argued and broke free of Sean's grip to head toward her.

Ronan stepped in between, still fighting the urge to blacken Michael's other eye. He could understand passion, but he didn't understand not taking precautions. Though even as he thought it, he remembered that Laura had become pregnant even *with* a condom being used.

Sean pulled Michael back, Patsy stood up to argue toe-to-toe with her daughter, and Sinead once again started crying. Ronan stood like a man lost in his own home and watched as Laura slipped from the room like a ghost.

Laura had had enough of the shouting and recriminations. Deciding no one would miss her if she disappeared, she took a chance and stepped through a pair of French doors leading onto a stone patio.

Instantly, the Irish wind pummeled her like a fist in a velvet glove. Icy, all enveloping, it wrapped itself around her and sent chills racing along her skin. And still it was easier to take than the drama she had just skipped out on.

Because the drama had hit too close to home, she thought, walking briskly across the patio. Her heels tapped musically against the stone as she set off blindly, not knowing where she was headed.

The sharp spicy scent of the chrysanthemums in the garden teased her nose and led her off the patio and onto a set of stone steps that wound through a garden that was mostly winter dormant. But she could see the bones of it and could easily imagine what it would be like in spring and summer.

Roses blooming, trellis standing over a white iron bench, alive with the morning glories that were now missing from the dark green vines. There was an herb garden and a few hardy dahlias still clinging to life at the edges of the garden.

Beyond lay a sweeping yard of green that sloped toward cliffs that echoed with the thunder of waves crashing ashore. She stood there, in the silence, letting her heartbeat ease, her mind empty and tried to release the fury that had prompted her escape.

But it clung to her insides, chilling her to the soul.

Shaking her head, she turned from the sea and looked up the rise of a rolling hill to where a round tower stood, ancient and alone. Without even thinking about it, she started for the tower, drawn by its solitude and the promise of peace.

She wasn't dressed for it. Her skin felt as icy as her heart as the wind continued its relentless pushing at her. Her heels sank into the soft ground until she was fighting for every step and still she went on, determined to reach the top. Halfway there, she heard the sighing of the wind as it slipped past the tower and through what she realized was an ancient cemetery.

Laura kept going even when she heard Deirdre's happy bark in the distance and coming closer. Swinging her hair back from her face, Laura stumbled, caught herself and went on, finally stepping out of her shoes altogether and carrying them in one hand. The long grass was soft and silky against her bare feet, but there were stones there as well and they scraped at her skin as she made her way higher.

Deirdre raced past her, barking in delight now, to have company on a run. Laura smiled in spite of the turmoil churning inside her until she heard an all-too-familiar voice coming from right behind her.

"You'll be frozen," Ronan warned, catching up to her and grabbing hold of her arm to stop her progress toward the tower.

"Doesn't matter," she argued, tugging free. "I'm fine."

"What're you doing, Laura?"

"I just needed to get out of that room." She glanced at him, then back to the tower that stood like a beacon. It was taller than she had thought. At least twenty feet high, and would have been even taller when it was built. The top of the thing was broken off, snapped in two as if a giant had reached down and broken it in a temper.

"And come to the cemetery?" he asked, whipping off his overcoat to drape it around her. "In your bare feet?"

"My heels kept sinking."

"Laura—"

She looked up at him then. "Leave me alone for a while, Ronan. Please."

"No." He cupped her face and the heat from his body touched her cold cheeks and swamped through her. "I'll not. If you're so determined to see the tower, I'll go with you."

Deirdre romped across the wide grassy expanse, chasing her own imagination across the field and up to where tilted tombstones stood in memory of those lost. There was a timelessness about this place, Laura thought. Centuries ago, this tower was built and the people then had been much the same as she and Ronan. The same wants and needs and fears and disappointments.

They'd lived and died and left their mark here, with this tower. With the tombstones.

What mark would she leave?

God, dark thoughts for a gray day on a windswept hill so far from home.

Ronan put one arm around her and drew her to him. His thick, Irish knit sweater was warm and smelled of him, making her want to cuddle close in spite of everything.

She didn't want to thank him. Didn't want to need

him beside her. Hated wanting even the warmth of his coat or his scent wafting up to her. But she did and couldn't hide that, at least from herself.

"It was a fine welcome to Ireland you got, wasn't it?" he asked, resting his chin on top of her head.

She didn't even comment on that because what could she say that wouldn't open her up to a conversation she wasn't interested in having. So instead, she half turned in his embrace and looked up at the stone tower, still standing proud.

"What were they for?"

"The round towers?" She felt him shrug. "No one knows for sure. Their name in Gaelic is *Cloigtheach* and in the old language it means 'belltower.' Some say it was for defense. That a lookout was perched high in the tower and if he saw the bloody Vikings coming back for another go-round, he'd sound the bell and the villagers would know to pack up what they could and run for it, while the warriors stayed behind to fight."

"What happened to this one?" she asked quietly, her voice nearly lost in the wind.

"Most likely it was destroyed in a long ago battle and what was left, time has whittled down."

"No graffiti though," she mused, staring up at the silent gray stones. If this were at home, she knew there would be spray-painted names and sayings and pictures all over it and that thought made her sad.

"No. We honor our past in Ireland and fight for our future."

She took a breath, looked up at him and asked flatly, "Like Sinead is trying to fight for hers?"

He held her more tightly as if afraid she might pull away from him, and Laura thought he was very attuned to her because that's exactly what she wanted to do.

"'Tis not the same, Laura. Sinead knew that marriage would be the end for her if there was a child. As did Michael."

"Forcing them to marry isn't right, Ronan." She whipped her hair back out of her eyes. "What if they're miserable together?"

"Most marriages end in misery from what I've seen," he said with a casual shrug that made her want to hit him with something heavy.

"And you'd wish that on Sinead?"

"You're not in America, Laura," he said patiently. "This is Ireland and though we've come a long way in the last few decades, a woman alone with a child still faces a hard road. Michael knew what he was risking. As did Sinead."

"Sex shouldn't come with a penalty."

"But it does, and everyone knows it." He blew out a breath then and added, "Besides that, I've told you. Things are different here."

"And yet," she said, "you seem the same. Still laying down orders expecting to be obeyed."

"You don't understand, and there's no reason you should." He fumed silently for a moment, then seemed to gather himself before saying, "No matter how it looked, Sinead's not being forced to do a damn thing. She's been after Michael since she was a girl, and she's finally landed him. She only wanted someone to tell her 'no' so that she could go and do what she liked. She's the most contrary girl in County Mayo. Always has been."

"So you were just doing her a favor?"

"In a way."

"And Sean hitting Michael in the eye, that was a good deed, too?"

Scrubbing both hands across his face, he muttered,

"The idiot man slept with a girl Sean and I both consider a little sister. Can you understand that we find that hard to deal with?"

Laura smiled to herself. "In fact, that's the one thing I completely understand."

"That's something then at least."

"You want her happy."

"I do," he admitted.

"Married."

"Married, for some, is the right thing," he muttered. "Or so I've heard."

"But not you."

He looked at her. "Not me."

"Right. So easy to stand back and order people to do what you won't do yourself. Or…is that what I would have been to you if I hadn't lost the baby?" she demanded. "A penance to be paid? A sacrifice bravely endured?"

He frowned at her. "Are you meaning would I have married you? Aye, I would have. For it's the right thing to do."

Stunned speechless, she could only look up at him and laugh in disbelief. "Do you even hear yourself? You believe marriage is a trap, yet you'd force that girl into its jaws and would have tried to drag me in, too."

"And would have, make no mistake," he grumbled.

Laura moved away and though she missed the heat of him, she couldn't be that close to him without wanting to kick him. "I wouldn't have married you, Ronan. I've no more interest in being some man's penance than Sinead does."

"And like Sinead, you'd have had no choice in the matter."

"Your arrogance is absolutely boundless."

"Is it arrogant to want to do what's right?" Temper flared on his features and glinted in his eyes. "If my child were still inside you, do you think I'd have let you go from me?"

A chill that had nothing to do with the icy wind crawled through Laura and sank bitter teeth into the edges of her soul. "I'm not pregnant now, Ronan, and you're still not letting me go. So what does that mean?"

Ronan looked at her, his jaw clenched, his eyes narrowed and his dark hair wind-tossed into a tangle. "It means I will let you go, Laura. But not yet."

He stomped off a few feet and whistled to Deirdre who was running too far away. As the dog careened back toward them, he looked at Laura.

"You know, I grew up in that house," he said, waving one arm at the manor behind them, "and never saw one reason to believe marriage was anything but a trap a man would chew his own foot off to escape."

She held her breath and listened. Watched. His eyes flashed with old pain and his mouth worked as if he'd tasted something bitter.

"My parents," he went on as if a dam had burst inside him and he couldn't stop the flow of words, "insisted they married for love, and yet spent every living minute tearing into each other. They were each of them miserable and were bound by the law and the church to remain so until death finally gave them—and me—some peace."

"All marriages aren't like that, Ronan," she finally said and reached down to stroke Deirdre's shaggy hair when the dog leaned into her.

"I'm not an idiot, you know," he said wryly, his temper draining away as easily as it had flashed into life. "I've seen some good ones. My friend Sam, a man as determined as I to remain single, is happy and about to be a father." He shook his head as if he didn't quite understand it, so he didn't see the flinch that must have shown on Laura's face.

She still felt the twinge of pain and memory when she thought of what she'd lost. But hearing Ronan now, she began to think that the pain she might have felt if the baby had lived, would have been worse.

He'd have expected marriage without love and that she wouldn't do.

"Those that make it work seem content enough," he continued. "But you are what you learn as a child, Laura. What I learned was to avoid marriage like the bloody plague." He stood in the gray light, with the wind tossing his hair into a tumble and looked directly into her eyes. "Don't look to me for love, I don't have it in me."

"You're wrong," she said and gave Deirdre one final pat. "You love your cousin. Sinead. Patsy."

"That's different."

It wasn't, but he couldn't see that. Laura had known him now for months. Had loved him in spite of how furious he made her at times. But he simply refused to be moved by even the chance that he might be wrong. He wouldn't risk love becoming what he'd seen as a child. How could they possibly ever breach the chasm between them?

"Love is love, Ronan," she said after a long moment. "You're capable of it. I've seen it in you. You're just too scared to risk it."

Insult etched onto his features in an instant. "If I am, I've a right to be. But either way, can't or won't, 'tis the same difference in the end."

The fact that he believed what he was saying tore

at Laura. She watched him, knowing that she loved him and realizing that they had no chance together. What they would share here in Ireland would be the last of it. When she went home, she'd be going alone and she wouldn't see Ronan again. Ever. Her heart simply couldn't take that kind of pain.

So she made a decision. The only one she could. She wouldn't have forever, so she would have *now*. Take Ronan as he was, for however long they were here in this place that was so beautiful it felt like a dream. Make memories that would keep her warm when the cold times came. Then, she would let him go.

Taking first one step, then two, she crossed to him and watched wariness flash in his eyes. She reached up, hooked her arms around his neck and went up on her toes. Looking into his eyes, she whispered, "You're wrong, Ronan. About all of it…"

"Laura, you must understand—"

"No, I don't have to. Not right now. Not here." Then she kissed him. She felt his hesitation at first, and then his hunger as he yielded to what each of them had been craving for too long.

He kissed her there, in the grayness of an Irish day, with Deirdre barking madly, the wind singing through the tombstones and in the distance, the heart of the sea beating with a steady drumroll.

Through her fury, through her misery, she fell into that kiss as if it meant her life. And for now, it did. Heart aching, mind reeling, she knew that when she did eventually go, she'd be leaving her heart behind.

And as his arms came around her, Laura's heart ached even as her mind whispered, *Remember this.*

Nine

The Pennywhistle Pub sat in the middle of the village of Dunley. It was small and noisy and filled with all those who needed to get away from their own homes for an hour or two to share conversation and music and a drink.

Laura loved it.

She'd been to pubs at home, of course. But in California the so-called "real" Irish pubs were nothing like this. There, the rooms were glossy, as if they were nothing more than a stage set, with potted ferns, piped in music coming down from overhead speakers and posters of Ireland tacked to the walls.

Here, the walls were stone, supported by what looked like ancient wooden beams, darkened by years of peat fire smoke. Rough-hewn tables that had probably sat in the same spot for a century or more, were lovingly polished and the bar itself, a long sweep of dark wood, gleamed in the overhead lights. Behind the bar, a television set on mute displayed a British soap opera, starring impossibly pretty people.

There were a half dozen or so tables in the pub, crowded with chairs and three booths along one wall where whole families, children included, gathered together. The smell of peat smoke layered over the crowd from the fireplace in one corner and the conversations and laughter around her rose and fell like the waves that stretched out behind the village.

Laura sipped at her beer and smiled when the owner of the pub, Danny Muldoon, came to their table. "Ronan, will you be staying for long this go round, or is it off to America again?"

"I'll be home awhile yet, Danny," Ronan said, with a long glance at Laura.

Danny's broad chest puffed out almost big enough to match the belly that strained the clean, white apron tied around his waist. His smile was beaming as he, too, looked at Laura. "If I'd known how lovely the lasses were across the foam, I might've taken myself off there long ago."

Ronan grinned. "Your Mary would probably be surprised to hear it."

"Ah, but I'd have taken her with me you see," Danny told him, "for she's the loveliest of them all." He winked at Laura. "Give us a call if you've need of another beer."

When he moved off into the crowd, stopping to chat with those he passed, Laura said, "You know everyone here, don't you?"

"Comes from growing up in one spot." He shrugged. "'Tis a small village after all."

The beer was cold, the pub was warm, and the look in Ronan's eyes when he turned to her was heated enough

to melt the strongest barricades she could erect around
her heart.

For two days, she'd lived in his world and watched
him with those who knew him best. Here, he was still
bossy and arrogant, but it was tempered with the real
caring he felt for the people. He'd told her once he didn't
have any family except Sean. But he was wrong, Laura
thought.

He had an entire village of family.

They all knew him. They all loved him, that was
plain to see, and they were all proud of what he'd made
of himself. Sitting here beside him, she was seeing a
whole new side of Ronan Connolly and her heart ached
at what she knew she'd soon be losing.

Since their first day in Ireland, since that afternoon
at the tower, Laura had spent every moment she could
with him. Days were filled with trips around the countryside, to the port city of Westport and to Galway so
she could see the Cosain offices and wander through
the shops. And every night, she lay in Ronan's bed,
wrapped in his arms, determined not to waste one instant of the time she had here.

"I saw the sketch you did of the round tower," Ronan
said, leaning in so that his voice was for her alone. "It
was lovely."

"Thank you." She hadn't bought paints in Galway,
as she wouldn't be here long enough to capture all that
she wanted to on canvas. Instead, she had settled for
a sketch pad and pencils, and told herself that when
she was home, she would take the time to paint them
all. Especially the round tower where she had willingly
crossed an emotional bridge, to take what joy she could
find. At home, she would bring back in oil the moments

she'd had here—and then she'd torture herself by hanging them all around her house.

Depressing thought.

She took a sip of beer and half listened to the conversation Ronan was having with another man about the coming winter and who in the village needed their roof fixed before the worst of it hit.

Her gaze locked on Ronan, she realized that he had no idea just how *much* he loved. He tried so hard to shut the emotion out of his life, but it was there, inside him, whether he recognized it or not. He didn't owe anyone here anything and yet, he was making plans to see that people who needed help were taken care of.

He was, she thought with a whip of anger that sliced through her internal misery, too stubborn to see the truth right in front of his eyes.

Still scowling, she turned her gaze to the door when it opened and smiled when Michael and Sinead entered the pub. The two of them looked happy, and Laura was glad to see that *someone* at least was getting what they wanted most.

"When's the wedding, Sinead?" someone called out from the back of the room.

"When the banns have been read," Michael shouted back and leaned down to kiss his bride-to-be.

Sinead laughed up at him, then stopped to talk to friends while Michael walked toward the hearth where two other young men his age waited, tuning up instruments.

"Michael's a musician?" she asked, leaning into Ronan while Michael pulled a violin from a case.

"He is," Ronan said, his breath brushing her skin. "And a fine one. He's a good future ahead of him and now that he's getting married and settling down, maybe he'll put some work into developing it."

Music jumped into life. Michael's fiddle sang with a fast tempo tune that had half the patrons singing and the other half leaping into fast, complicated step dancing that would have made the Riverdance company hang their heads in shame.

Ronan draped one arm around Laura's shoulders, and she leaned into him, smiling. One more memory, she thought, and lay her head on his shoulder.

For the next few days, all was peaceful and so Ronan's internal warning system was on red alert. He was waiting, he thought, for the skies to open and all hell to rain down on him. Nothing could be this good for long.

His time with Laura had been a revelation to him. She'd flung herself into village life and the easy pace of things in Ireland as if born to it. At home, in California, she seemed like everyone else there, always in a hurry. But here, she found time to sit and sketch, to work with Patsy in the kitchen and to stroll the beach with him just to watch the waves crashing to shore.

And the people here, *his* people, loved her.

He saw it with Sinead, when she and Laura sat before the fire, talking about American music and Hollywood, which fascinated Sinead to no end at all. He saw it with Patsy, who traded her recipe for Irish soda bread for Laura's on how best to make spaghetti sauce. He even saw it with Sean, who kept finding reasons to stop by the manor, and in the village of Dunley, where she'd already made friends.

Everywhere she went, Laura carved out a place for herself—as she had with him.

Oh, Ronan didn't want to acknowledge it, but it was becoming damned difficult to ignore. She had etched her presence onto every corner of his home. He knew that years from now, he would still be walking into the front parlor and be able to see Laura, curled up on the sofa with a book in her hands and Deirdre at her feet.

And that didn't even bring to mind the images he had of Laura in his bed. Moonlight across her skin, the shimmer of lamplight against her blond hair. The sigh of her breath when she lay across him in the middle of the night because she was cold. The heat of her body pressed along his and the cry of her voice when he emptied himself into her.

All of these and more were driving Ronan round the bend.

Because though his world seemed peaceful, beneath the surface, everything around him was shifting and changing and damned if he liked knowing that.

"We've another request for a guard from the Baileys in Dublin."

"What?" Ronan looked up at Molly O'Hara, serving as his assistant while Brian was still away in California. Frowning, he shook his head, tried to remember what they had been talking about before his mind wandered. And, he thought with a frown, until Laura had invaded his life, he'd had no problems with concentration. "Right. Yes. The Baileys. Have you explained to them that it'll be a week or more?"

"I have," she admitted with a sigh. "And they're none too happy about the wait. They've offered to double the signing fee if you can get them an agent faster."

John Bailey, Ronan thought, quickly reviewing what he knew of the potential customer. Industrial tycoon, single, Bailey made many trips overseas, running his various businesses and he wanted personal protection. The problem was, they had no one free at the moment.

When Sam Travis certified the new recruits though, Ronan thought the former marine, Cobb, would be the perfect fit for Bailey.

"I'll take care of it," Ronan said. "Leave me his file. We've a new batch of guards graduating from training within the week, Bailey will either wait for one of them or not, as he chooses."

"As you wish," she said and handed over the file. "Unless there's anything else you need, it's late so I'll be leaving now and see you again on Monday morning?"

"Fine, Molly. Thanks." When she was gone, Ronan tossed the file onto his desk, then swiveled his chair around to stare out at the night over Galway city and the bay beyond. He'd stayed later than usual, and now he saw the sweep of stars across the sky and was forced to admit to a truth. Burying himself in work didn't help. Pretending that he was in no hurry to return home to Laura didn't change reality.

Ronan realized that for the first time in memory, he didn't want to be at work.

He wanted to be home.

Where Laura waited.

He hungered for her, damn it. He had wanted her to come to Ireland with him as a means of making *her* desires quicken. Instead, it was he himself doing the suffering. No matter how much he touched her, it wasn't enough. He craved more until his body felt as tight as a bodhrán drum.

Ronan had wanted *her* on the razor's edge, not himself.

When, he asked himself, had she become...vital?

And what was he to do about it?

He didn't want her to leave, he knew that. Though it had nothing to do with love, as well he knew. It was a problem for sure, but all problems had solutions if you looked hard enough and were willing to work toward compromise. Laura wanted love and marriage. He couldn't give her that. But surely there was something else he could offer in its stead.

Possibilities raced through his mind.

At home, he found her in his bedroom, warm and lovely in his bed, and Ronan knew he'd like nothing better than to come home to her every night for the rest of his life. And he would, he vowed. If he played his cards right, if he could convince her to see things his way, they could each have what it was they wanted.

Ronan stripped quietly, quickly, and went to her, sliding beneath the blood-red duvet and gathering her in close.

She sighed and flowed against him, one leg sliding across his, one arm draped over his chest, her head pillowed on his shoulder. Her hair felt like silk and smelled like summer.

"You worked late," she murmured.

"I did," he said, kissing her forehead, sliding one hand along her spine. "Had a few things to work out in my mind."

She tipped her head back to look up at him and a slice of moonlight slanted across her features, shadowing her eyes, making her skin seem to glow. "Did you get everything settled?"

"You know me," he said softly.

"I do." A smile curved her mouth and his breath caught. That brilliant smile, freely given and so filled with joy, jolted through him like a hammer against rock.

He felt her power over him and told himself that it meant nothing. Only that he'd a fondness for her. And for the magic they made together.

But even he was having a hard time believing that. Determinedly, he closed his mind to the thoughts clamoring for his attention.

"I've no wish for talking at the moment," he said, rolling over until she lay beneath him. He went up on one elbow to look into her eyes and used the tips of his fingers to smooth back a strand of blond hair.

"I don't really feel like talking, either," she admitted and lifted one hand to trace the curve of his mouth with her fingers.

"That's good then," he whispered and dipped his head for a kiss.

Every time he kissed her it was as if it were the first time. The same sensations crowded inside him. Light and heat and a powerful explosion of electricity that shot through his mind and body and left him breathless. She was a hunger in his blood and Ronan knew she always would be.

He tore his mouth from hers and trailed his lips down the line of her throat and farther, letting the scent of her envelop him. He moved until he found her breasts and the dark pink tips of her nipples. He tasted one, then the other, swirling his tongue over their sensitive points until Laura sighed with pleasure and murmured his name.

Her talented hands moved over his back, tugged at his shoulders and finally cupped his cheek and guided his face back to hers.

"You're lovely," he said softly, loving the way moonlight caressed her.

"You're prejudiced," she countered.

"No." He bent to kiss her again, taking his time with it, giving them both the sensations they craved. His chest tight, mind crowded with thoughts and feelings he couldn't explore, he said only, "I'm not. You're the loveliest thing I've ever seen."

"Ronan—"

He moved over her, pushing his body into hers on one long slide. Instantly, he was lost in the heat of her. He groaned, from deep in his throat and set a rhythm she moved to match. Again and again, he took her, each time, driving them higher, closer to the end that waited for them, and when he heard her cry, felt her body tremble, he at last allowed himself to follow.

His gaze locked with hers as the world shattered around them and Ronan knew that without her, nothing would ever be the same for him.

A few minutes later, with Laura cuddled against him, Ronan decided it was the perfect time to tell her the plan he'd come up with. "You know I told you that I stayed late at work, figuring a few things out?"

"Uh-huh." She sounded warm and sated and comfortable.

"Well," he said softly, "I've decided what needs to be done."

"About what?"

"About us."

That had her attention, he thought as she pushed up from his chest to look at him. Her hair hung in a tangle around her face and shoulders, but her eyes were clear and focused on his.

"Meaning what exactly?"

"Meaning," Ronan told her with a smile, "I think we should be married."

"What?" Frowning now, she sat up straight, the duvet

pooled in her lap as her hair fell forward to lay across the tops of her breasts.

Idly, he lifted one hand to toy with one of her nipples, but she batted his hand aside. "What are you talking about? Marriage? You said marriage was a trap."

"It could be, if you went into it all wide-eyed and in love and expecting roses every day," he said. "But if we went into this as partners—as *friends,* even—we could each have what it is we want most."

"Friends."

"More than," he assured her, pushing himself up higher and stuffing a pillow behind his back. "It would be the best of all possible worlds, Laura," he said, slightly surprised that she hadn't jumped at his proposal. This was what she had wanted, wasn't it?

Taking her hand in his, he rubbed his thumb across her knuckles, unconsciously soothing her. "I never thought to ask a woman to be mine forever. But with you, it's different."

"Different."

He frowned a little. Her lack of enthusiasm worried him, but he was in too deep now to back away, even if he had wanted to. "We're a good team, Laura. We get along nicely. We're great in bed together. We could be happy."

"Happy."

Scowling now, he blurted, "Are you only going to repeat my words? Have you nothing to say? I've never asked anyone to share my life before you."

"What am I supposed to say, Ronan? Have you figured that out, too?"

"Didn't think I'd have to," he admitted, "though if I had, it would have been different than this."

Actually, he'd seen it all so clearly in his mind. Him making his very logical, clearly thought out proposal.

Her, throwing herself into his arms with a happy cry and a resounding *Yes, I'll marry you, Ronan!*

Perhaps, he thought, she just couldn't believe how nicely he'd worked it all out. How he had been able to see that she was right and how good they were together.

"And anywhere in this little scenario of yours," Laura asked, "did the word *love* come up at all?"

"No, it didn't and why would it, I ask you?" Her features froze so he spoke again, quickly. "This is more of a partnership. More in the way of a contract. Isn't it enough that I desire you? That I admire so much about you? That I bloody *like* you?"

"No," she said, dragging the duvet up until she held it like a shield in front of her. "It isn't. I want more than desire from a husband. I want love."

"Damn it, Laura, be reasonable."

"Why should I? I want a family, Ronan. Children."

"As do I," he snapped and shoved one hand through his hair, fingers scraping along his skull. "I admit, I hadn't thought of it until you told me of our lost child, but since then, the loss has haunted me. I keep thinking about that baby and what might have been."

Her fingers plucked at the duvet as she whispered, "So do I."

Ronan reached for her, taking her hands in his. "We could have children together, Laura. Build a family and neither of us has to risk something so ethereal as *love*. Marry me, Laura. Live with me here. We'll bring Beast to Ireland and we can all have what we want."

She didn't speak and that gave him hope. She hadn't said no, so maybe, if he gave her the time she'd need to see that he was right about this, it would all work out in the end.

"Will you think about it, Laura?" His words came

softly, but his grip on her hands was tight enough to feel her tremble. "Will you do that at least?"

"I'll think about it, Ronan, but I won't make you any promises."

"That'll do, for now," he said and pulled her in close, wrapping his arms around her as if determined to hold her tightly enough to prevent her escaping him.

The following day, he took her to Dublin, where they had an elegant dinner at an amazing restaurant. He watched her over the candlelight and when his eyes flared with passion, Laura's heart trip-hammered in her chest.

His "proposal" continued to run through her mind and Laura was torn in two over it. He'd offered her the chance to stay. To be with him. To have children with him. To make the family she wanted so badly.

All she would have to do is give up on love.

And that she couldn't do.

She'd settled once before, she reminded herself, with Thomas. And without real love, even their engagement hadn't lasted. What chance would a marriage have if it didn't start out the right way? Besides, how could she marry him, loving him as she did, all the while knowing he wouldn't love her back?

Oh, she hadn't told him yet, because she didn't want to waste what little time she had left with him in arguments that wouldn't change anything. She needed love. He wouldn't give it. So there was no chance for compromise, no matter what the great and powerful Ronan Connolly might think.

God, she would miss him.

Her memories were piling up inside her, and she knew, that as wonderful as they were, they would choke her with misery once she was home and alone again. Yet she couldn't begrudge this time with Ronan. Couldn't help but be glad he had blackmailed her into this trip.

After dinner, they walked the crowded streets, hand in hand. She heard traditional Irish music pouring from the dozens of pubs they passed in the Castlebar district. There was a sense of urgency here, in Dublin, that the village of Dunley didn't have. It was bright and shiny and filled with tourists even so late in the season. She heard snatches of accents from around the world—American, British, German and more—and yet, with her hand in Ronan's, she felt as if she belonged there.

They stood on one of the lovely bridges and stared down into the river Liffey, looking like a silver thread in the moonlight, winding its way through the city.

And he kissed her there, sliding his fingers through her hair, holding her while he took his time about tasting her, driving her body into a mad gallop of passion. Another memory made, she told herself, as the city and all of the people fell away.

When he ended the kiss, he leaned his forehead against hers and whispered, "We've a two-hour drive to get back to Dunley. Shall we go home, or get a hotel for the night?"

The scent of the sea floated past them on a brisk wind, fluttering the hem of her dress and ruffling Ronan's hair. She was far from the home she'd made for herself in California. But the home of her heart was within reach and she suddenly wanted nothing more than to be there. With Ronan.

"Let's go home," she said.

He grinned. "Good answer."

Then he draped one arm around her shoulders and together, they left the city behind.

Ten

Maeve Carrol was seventy years old and more stubborn than two rocks. The woman had been Ronan's nanny when he was a boy and was somehow under the impression he hadn't yet grown up. She gave him the look he remembered from his childhood, and he sighed.

Ronan was at the end of his tether. But it wasn't dealing with Maeve that had him feeling as though there was a spike going through his head. It was Laura. As hardheaded as the old woman standing patiently before him, Laura refused to see reason. Refused to even discuss his proposal. What the hell more did she want from him?

He kept expecting her to suddenly see he was right. To throw her arms around him and say yes. That she'd marry him and stay here, in Dunley, where, he told himself, she bloody well belonged.

He was willing, wasn't he, to make a life and children with her? It was more than he'd ever offered any other woman. Couldn't she see that? Was the woman really so blind as to ignore what they might have together for the sake of her pride?

It seemed so. After their evening in Dublin, she'd begun to close herself off to him. There was a distance in her smile, in her touch and a part of him worried that no matter how he tried to make her stay, she was already preparing to leave.

The woman was making him crazy.

He glanced over at Laura now, wearing her jeans and a thick cable knit sweater in a soft oatmeal color. Her blond hair hung down on her shoulders and her smile was for Maeve alone.

His chest ached, and he rubbed one fist against it. Wasn't his heart. He knew that because he wasn't—and *couldn't be*—in love. Asking for trouble that was and God knew he'd seen enough of that in his lifetime already. But he cared for her, that he could admit freely. So why wasn't that enough?

Why did it have to be so damned complicated, this thing he and Laura shared? Why couldn't they keep it simple, untangled by emotion and guided instead by the logic he saw so plainly? Wasn't it easy enough to see that he just wanted to be with her? That they enjoyed being together? That they liked each other? Why must they make more of it than that? Why did she need words that choked in his throat? Why couldn't the woman see that he was offering her more than he'd ever thought to offer anyone?

Marriage under the conditions he'd laid out so thoughtfully could be a blessing rather than the curse he'd been buried under as a child. Why couldn't she bloody *see* it?

Temper chewing at him, Ronan took a breath and told

himself to give her time to think. Time to realize that what they could have was too good to turn her back on.

Meanwhile...

"Maeve, it's a sodding roof," Ronan said, patience wearing thin in his voice. "If you don't let me replace it, when the rains come this winter, you might as well be sleeping outside for all the cover you'll have. You'll wash away to sea on a tide of your own stubbornness."

The older woman lifted an eyebrow at that and stiffened her spine until her whole five feet two inches of height looked formidable. "You'll mind your tongue with me, Ronan Matthew Connolly."

Laura watched, amused and touched, as Ronan bit back the temper she could see sparking in him and said only, "Yes, ma'am."

"When I need a new roof," Maeve told him, with a fast glance at her white-washed cottage with the bright blue door, "I'll let you know. Until then, you can patch the holes."

Over breakfast that morning, Ronan had told Laura exactly what would happen when they went to Maeve's cottage. She had been his nanny when he was a boy, and he looked out for her, but he claimed she didn't make it easy.

Laura wouldn't make things easy for him, either. His proposal still echoed with a dull thud in her heart. She'd done as he asked and had thought about it. But she always came back to the same conclusion. Marry as friends. She'd never heard anything so stupid in her life. It amazed her that he'd actually gotten the words out at all, not to mention the fact that he'd looked so proud of himself for finding a solution to their situation.

She imagined he had thought of his proposal as quite the compromise. Give Laura what she wants without having to give anything truly important of himself. His body, yes. Children, sure. But his heart, Ronan would keep locked away in a drawer somewhere.

Hardheaded, close-minded, wonderful man that he was, he couldn't even see that with his offer, he was cheating them both out of something special. Something once-in-a-lifetime special.

It was going to break her heart in two to leave him, but she didn't have a choice. Not anymore.

"There are more holes in that roof than there are shingles," Ronan said, shattering her thoughts.

"Then you'd best get busy," Maeve told him, blithely brushing aside his rising temper.

He threw his hands high in defeat and stomped off, after giving Laura a *What did I tell you?* glance.

Alone with the older woman, Laura followed her to a worn wooden bench beneath a tree, then sat down beside her. "You know, he really wants to put a new roof on for you."

"Oh, I know, but this one will do another year." Maeve patted Laura's hand. "Always a generous one, is Ronan. He's a good boy, mind, but he never could figure out how to take no for an answer."

"He does like to get his own way," Laura muttered, watching as he strode across the roof, balancing a heavy weight of shingles on one shoulder.

"And why wouldn't he?" Maeve clucked her tongue and shook her head. "Raised by those who should have known better, to be as self-sufficient as he could. He was making his own decisions at ten and was as hard to move from them as a boulder from the mud."

Here was a source who might be able to give Laura some real insight into Ronan. Carefully, she said, "He's told me about his parents. That they were miserable together."

"That they were," Maeve agreed with a sigh. "Two less suited people I've never known. Butting heads together like two rams fighting for the same herd."

Laura sighed in sympathy for the boy he'd been and looked up at the man, kneeling on a roof, hammering shingles into place for a woman who needed—but didn't want to need—the help. He was so damned stubborn. Insisting he didn't know how to love when the proof that he *did* was right there in front of him.

Laura *felt* the love he had for her when they were together, but she wasn't going to settle for less than hearing the words. If he never admitted what he felt, how could he really commit to her? To a life together?

She remembered his proposal again, offering her what he could but withholding what they both needed and she tried to understand, in spite of the pain. But why did he have to be so thickheaded about this? He did love her. He just refused to see it.

"It must have been hard on Ronan."

"Oh aye, it was," Maeve agreed. "Ronan was, most often, caught between the two, torn always in his loyalties until finally he turned from them both. And who could blame him?"

"But he had you."

"He did. He also had Sean and his mother, plus his friends in the village and Patsy Brennan, bless her." Maeve frowned. "But always there was an emptiness in him where that love he'd missed should have been. Still and all, he grew up fine, with a good heart."

"He did," Laura said. "But it's his hard head I have a problem with."

Maeve laughed. "Well, that's not a surprise, either. Always was as proud as a bishop and as sure of himself."

"And absolutely convinced that he doesn't know how to love," Laura blurted. She cringed a little as soon as the words left her. She hadn't meant to say that aloud.

Maeve blinked at her, eyes wide as she shook her head in denial. "But that's nonsense."

"Thank you." Laura smiled sadly. "I know it is. Unfortunately, Ronan believes it, absolutely."

Maeve squeezed Laura's hand. "And you're after changing his mind."

"I tried," she admitted, feeling that heaviness in her heart that she was getting so accustomed to.

"Ah. You'd better luck turning back the tide with a wall of sand."

"I suppose so." Sitting here in the shade of the tree with the sound of Ronan's hammer tapping away like an angry heartbeat, she realized that she'd needed this talk with a woman who also loved Ronan.

"What is it that's tearing at you, love?" Maeve's voice was gentle, her hand on Laura's firm and steady.

"I really tried to reach him, but I failed, I guess."

"You love him."

"I do," Laura confessed, "not that it matters."

"It's *all* that matters."

"Not if he's too stubborn to ever admit that he loves me, too," Laura said, glaring at Ronan now. His back was turned to her as he wrestled free an old, rotten shingle then sent it sailing over his shoulder to the ground. "I *know* he does," she whispered, more to herself than to Maeve. "I can see it in his eyes. But he won't admit to it. Won't let himself feel it. Won't let *us* share it."

"Don't give up on him, Laura," Maeve said, her grip on Laura's hand tightening. "He's not an easy man, but he is a good one. I've seen the way he looks at you and aye, there's love there. He just hasn't found a way to accept it yet. He will. I know he will."

"Maybe." Laura sighed heavily as she watched Ronan grab another shingle and hammer it into place. She hated that her anger was sliding away into misery. Anger was so much easier to deal with.

"But Maeve, I can't simply stay here indefinitely and hope that he figures it out some day. That would kill me by inches, I think. No. I have to go home. While I still can."

With the hammering pounding away and the sigh of the sea in the background, Maeve frowned and watched the man she'd loved since he was a boy and thought that maybe it was time for another lesson.

Monday morning saw Ronan off to work and Laura set to do what she had to. Leave him while she still could.

She felt badly, sneaking off this way, but she never would have been able to say goodbye to him face-to-face. One look into his eyes and she'd forget all about wanting more and learn to settle for what she could get.

But it wouldn't be enough, in the end. And sooner or later, she'd come to resent him for holding back. So, better like this, she assured herself, zipping her suitcase closed. Better for both of them.

She had a reservation on one of Sean's Irish Air jets to take her to Heathrow in London and from there she'd book a flight home to California. Wryly, she smiled as she took one last look around Ronan's bedroom. The room they had shared for almost two weeks.

The wide bed with the dark red duvet. The windows that opened out onto a view of the garden she would never see blossom in the springtime. The two wide, leather chairs in front of the now cold hearth where she and Ronan had cuddled to watch the flames dance in the darkness.

"Oh, God…" Laura swallowed the knot of misery in her throat and forced it into the cold hard shell of her heart.

She had built enough memories in the last week or more to last her a lifetime. It would have to be enough.

With the wheels of her suitcase humming against the wood floor, she walked from the room, and closed the door behind her.

She didn't look back.

That odd sense of something being…off…stayed with Ronan.

He couldn't seem to shake it and when he tried, it settled in deeper. Since the night of his proposal, Laura had seemed quieter. More thoughtful. That distance he'd felt coming from her at Maeve's cottage had grown more pronounced. He told himself it was only because she was seriously considering his offer. Thinking about what they could have, the two of them, if only she were willing to bend.

"Must she be so damned contrary?" he muttered in disgust. "Can't she see that all she needs to do is give just a bit and we can have what we want?"

The echo of his words slapped back at him in the quiet of his office and for the first time, he realized that Laura had been the one to bend all along. She hadn't wanted an affair, but had gone into one with him because she'd cared for him.

He had seen it from the beginning, the shine in her eyes, the dreams of a future. Wasn't that what had chased him off in the first place? Damned humiliating to admit, even to himself.

She had taken in his dog and yes, held him hostage, but only because she rightly thought that Beast had deserved a better owner than Ronan had been.

Scowling now, he thought back, going over every moment with Laura. She had worked with him, arguing all the way, but had showed him house after house, hoping to find the one he wanted—when the truth was, all he had wanted was more time with her.

And finally, she'd come home to Ireland with him. All right, yes, he'd blackmailed her into it, but once she was here, with him, she'd thrown herself into the moment, not holding anything back from him. He'd felt love in her touch, tasted it in her kiss and knew that he didn't want to live without it.

She was unique, he thought, stalking toward the wide window that overlooked the city and the stretch of ocean that spilled out toward the sky at the horizon. A blue sky and thick white clouds framed the picture of Ireland today, but he saw none of it. All he could see, was *her*.

Strong and soft, loving and stubborn, kind and generous. Laura was smart and funny and ambitious and talented and damned if she wasn't everything he'd ever wanted in a woman and more.

"Bend," he muttered, slapping both hands to the wall at either side of the window and leaning in. His own reflection shone back at him and he read the shadows of frustration in his own eyes. "Will you ask her for even more? Or will you at last admit to what you feel? What you know?" Staring at the man in the glass, Ronan asked, "Can you risk it? Can you afford to *not* risk it?"

A knock at the door sounded and he turned, grateful for the interruption. Molly walked into the office. "A Mrs. Carrol is here to see you, sir."

"Maeve Carrol? Here in the office?"

"Yes, sir, she doesn't have an appointment but—"

"I'm right here, girl, you don't have to speak around me," Maeve said, stepping into the room.

"Sorry, Mr. Connolly," Molly told him with a wince. "I did ask her to wait—"

"She did, but I've no time to waste sitting out there waiting." Maeve stood as stiff and straight as a soldier and looked, Ronan thought, like an elfin sentinel.

"It's all right." He looked at his assistant and nodded. Coming around from behind his desk, he walked to Maeve, and taking her arm, led her into his office. "That'll be all, Molly. Just close the door on your way out."

When his assistant was gone, Ronan settled Maeve in a chair and then perched on the edge of his desk to look down at her. He couldn't have been more astonished. To the best of his knowledge, Maeve hadn't left Dunley but for the occasional trip into Westport in more than a decade.

Which meant her visit didn't herald happy news. "Are you all right?"

"I'm fine, fine."

One worry out of the way. "What's the matter then, Maeve? I don't think you've been to Galway in years."

"I haven't, no," she agreed, folding both hands atop her big black purse. "And haven't missed it. The traffic and the crowds are not to my liking."

He smiled in spite of the turmoil inside him. Here, he thought, was one of the pillars of his life. Maeve Carrol, Patsy Brennan...

Idiot.

Laura had said much the same to him, hadn't she? Told him that he knew all about love. That he had plenty of it in him to share because she'd seen it with those already in his life. He hadn't wanted to hear her. Hadn't wanted to admit to himself that he loved Laura Page. Because to acknowledge that meant that he was risking the loss of that love. The possibility of leaving his heart and soul open to be carved up into tiny pieces.

But if he never risked it, he never won, did he? There's a line of thinking he hadn't considered before, and damn it all, Ronan liked to win. How could he have cheated himself out of the greatest win of all? To hold Laura's heart and to trust her to hold his…there couldn't be a greater prize.

He loved her.

Odd, but that thought didn't make him quail and want to run for the hills as it once had. Though it shamed him to think he'd once had such cowardly thoughts at all. Instead, the knowledge that he loved her gave him a steadiness he'd sorely lacked these past few weeks. It was as if the world had stopped tipping wildly beneath his feet.

As if he'd discovered his place and had no more need to wander about pretending he didn't care that he was alone.

All he had to do now was go home, tell Laura that he was done being pigheaded and tell her that she bloody well would marry him. His mind hadn't changed on that, but he could tell her he loved her, and he would. He wouldn't go blurting out something big like that though. He'd need to take her somewhere special, he told himself. When he finally opened himself to love and wanted to lay his heart at his woman's feet, then he damned well would make an occasion of it.

At the round tower, he thought, with the past surrounding them and the future theirs to grab.

It would be perfect.

"Have you nodded off then?" Maeve asked, giving him a shove. "I've come all the way to the city to see you, the least you could do is pay attention."

Laughing, he came back to himself and focused his gaze on the small woman in front of him. "You're absolutely right. I was just…coming to a decision is all."

"Is that right?" Eyes gleaming with speculation, she looked him over.

"It is," he said with a grin. The woman's curiosity was piqued, but she'd just have to wait as Laura should be the first to know that he'd come to his senses at long last.

"So, what is it I can do for you, Maeve?" he asked, studying the woman who had been his world from birth to the age of ten.

She frowned at him. "You can wake up to the truth of things before it's too late to set them right."

"What's that supposed to mean?"

"It means, I've come to speak with you about Laura."

"Laura? What's wrong?" He pushed off the edge of the desk. "Has something happened to her?"

"She looked fine when last I saw her," Maeve told him.

A trickle of unease dripped through his system. "When last you—but she said she was going to spend the day—one moment."

He stopped, scrubbed one hand across the back of his neck, then shoved that hand into his pants pocket. Something was wrong. Something was *very* wrong. Looking down at the prim little woman in front of him, Ronan said flatly, "She said she was spending the day with *you*. That you'd agreed to let her sketch your portrait."

"Aye, well," Maeve told him with a sniff, "she didn't have time for that, did she? She'd a plane to catch after all."

"A *plane?*"

"'Tis what I said. I know you're not deaf."

"Maeve, tell me—"

"She looked as though she'd had a good cry for herself when she stopped at my cottage to tell me goodbye."

"Goodbye?"

"Are you only going to repeat words to me, Ronan? Or are you going to hear me out?"

That got his attention. It was very similar to what he'd said to Laura just a few nights ago when he'd laid out his reasonable, very logical proposal. The one that he wished now he could call back and wipe from her mind. A fool is what he was.

The woman offered him love, and he offered her friendship.

It was a wonder she hadn't coshed him over the head with something heavy.

Then Maeve's words echoed inside him.

Laura had a plane to catch?

She was leaving Ireland?

Leaving him?

Ronan got a grip on the wild racing of his thoughts and forced himself to focus on the woman staring at him. Her pale green eyes were narrowed on him in a way he hadn't seen since he was nine years old and had broken his mother's favorite vase with a kick of a football.

"I'm listening, Maeve," he told her. "What did she

say? Where did she go? And by all that's holy *why* did she go?"

That last question wasn't hard to answer though. She'd left because he'd given her no choice. His compromise was all one-sided, expecting her to give up all that she was and in exchange, he offered her a legal contract of a marriage.

Idiot.

Carefully, Maeve worked the latch on her purse and pulled out a thin, ivory-colored envelope. Ronan recognized the stationery as the same as what he kept in his desk at home. That trickle of unease became a slippery flood as he took it and tore open the flap. He read the brief note in a second or two.

> *Ronan,*
> *I'm sorry to leave this way, but if I had looked you in the eye, I wouldn't have been able to say goodbye. I never would have found the courage to go. And I have to go. I can't stay with a man who won't let himself love me.*
> *I'll never forget my time here, with you. And when you do come back to Cosain in California, I'll return Beast to you, too. I don't want you to be alone in your beautiful new house.*
> *Please remember that I love you,*
> *Laura*

He stared down at the damned letter, his gaze moving over and over the words, and still he didn't believe it. A yawning emptiness opened up inside him and promptly coated over with a skim of ice. His fist crumpled the paper and held tight as though, if he squeezed hard enough, he could make the words disappear.

When Ronan knew he could speak without the hard knot in his throat strangling him, he muttered, "She's gone? She left?"

"Seems clear to me she has," Maeve told him, her gaze fixed on him as if trying to read his heart, his mind.

Good luck to her with that, he thought frantically. Even *he* couldn't make sense of all of the thoughts and emotions charging through him.

She's gone.

"Off to the airport she went, to catch one of Sean's flights to London she says and from there on to home."

Home. Where she'd be an ocean away from him.

"And what'll you do about it?"

His gaze shot to Maeve's. The canny old woman was watching him, knowing that what she'd told him would either make him or break him. Well, it had done the former. He'd already made up his mind to have Laura and damned if he'd let this stop him.

"I'll stop her," he said. "Then I'll bring her back here, kiss her senseless and convince her to marry me."

Maeve gave him a sharp nod. "That ought to do it. You've a bit of time yet. I had Aidan Muldoon drive her to the airport and told him to get lost on the way. She'll miss her plane. The rest is up to you."

"You're a brilliant woman, Maeve Carrol."

"I know. What're you standing here for? Don't you have a plane to catch?"

"I do indeed." He bent down, gave her a hard kiss on the cheek, then grinned at her. "Bless you, Maeve. I'll have my assistant arrange for a ride home for you."

Maeve settled back in her chair as Ronan grabbed up his suit coat and strode from the room, hollering for Molly as he went.

"Well, now," Maeve said to herself with a pleased smile, "if my boy can't convince the girl that she's loved, no one can. Yes, well worth the trip to Galway, I think."

Then she stood and followed Molly out to the waiting car.

Eleven

By the time Laura arrived at the airport, her plane was long gone. And when she tried to book another, she was told there was a problem with her passport. Honestly, she'd never been more frustrated in her life.

The industrial gray walls of the security office were closing in on her, Laura thought. She was nervous enough to need to pace but there wasn't enough room to accomplish it, so instead, she stayed glued to the chair she'd been in for nearly—she checked the wall clock again—*two hours*.

"I don't understand," Laura complained for what had to be the fiftieth time. "*Why* am I being held here?"

"As I said, there's a problem with your passport, miss," the airport security chief answered, "and until it's settled, you'll simply have to wait."

"But what kind of problem?"

"That I don't know," he said with a smile. "Can I get you another cup of tea?"

"No, thank you. What you can do, is let me leave. I have to make my connecting flight in London."

"Not until things are sorted out, miss."

Sorted out. How could they sort something out when they hadn't even told her what was wrong? But then, nothing had gone right for Laura from the moment she left Maeve's cottage. She had hired Danny Muldoon's son Aidan to drive her to the airport, but the boy had gotten so turned around they'd been completely lost and she'd missed her flight on Irish Air.

If she didn't get another one soon, she'd miss her flight out of Heathrow as well.

"Am I under arrest for something?"

"No one's said anything about arrests, now have they? There's no need to be upset, miss. I'm sure this will be taken care of as soon as himself arrives."

Suspicion curled in her belly. "Himself? Who's himself?"

"The one who'll straighten this out, miss." The burly security guard had closely cropped red hair, an explosion of freckles on his round face and guileless blue eyes.

Laura narrowed her own gaze on him. Something was going on here. And it wasn't just the security guard. Aidan Muldoon, getting lost in a county where he'd lived his whole life? Laura missing her plane? Unable to book another one? Seemed wildly unlikely unless...

"There you are."

She closed her eyes and took a deep breath as the sound of that deep, oh-so-familiar voice echoed in her mind, her heart. Her heartbeat quickened as she turned around to look up into Ronan's eyes. "You were behind all of this, weren't you?"

He only glanced at her before turning his gaze to the security chief. "Thanks for this, Eddie. Could we have a moment?"

"Sure you can, Ronan." Affably, the man walked around his desk and stepped outside, leaving Laura alone with the man she wanted to kick.

When the guard was gone, Laura shouted, "You know each other!"

"Sure. Eddie Flanagan lives in Dunley. His mother, Frances, runs the post office. I grew up with Eddie."

"How *nice* for you." Ready to explode now, Laura fired a hard look at him. "So basically what? You called the airport and got your old buddy Eddie to do you a favor by arresting me?"

"You weren't arrested," he said. "Just detained until I could get here from Galway."

"You had no right," she snapped and grabbed her purse. "I'm leaving Ireland. Leaving *you,* and you can't stop me."

"Oh, I can and all," he purred, that voice of his rumbling through the tiny room and dancing along every one of her already twitchy nerve endings.

She whipped her hair back and glared at him. "Just go away, Ronan."

"I'll not."

Laura grabbed the handle of her suitcase and drew it up to its telescoping length. "You shouldn't be here." She stopped and stared at him. "*Why* are you here?" A second or two later, what must have happened clicked. "Maeve," she said, nodding to herself. "Maeve told you."

"Aye, she did."

"The traitor," Laura murmured, and thinking back,

remembered that it was Maeve who had arranged for Aidan to drive Laura to the airport. It had all been a trick. A way to stall her until Ronan could find her.

"I should have known," she said. "Of course they'd all be on your side."

"You left me a *note,*" he accused.

Disgusted at how badly her nicely laid out plan had failed, she muttered, "It was better. Easier."

"Easier than what?"

"Than looking into your eyes and trying to say goodbye."

"'Twas cowardly, Laura," he said. "Sneaking off, trying to be gone before I knew anything about it. Before I could *do* anything about it."

"Cowardly?" she countered and welcomed the first, hot flash of temper that jolted through her. "As cowardly as couching a marriage proposal as a contract between *friends?* That kind of cowardly, Ronan?"

He winced, and she was glad to know the barb had hit home. She'd hugged that ridiculous proposal to her breast for days now and it was good to finally tell him how she felt about it.

"That's a word I'd never thought to apply to myself," he admitted softly with a shake of his head. "But the sad truth is, you're right. It was cowardly. But you've done no better here. So we're quite the match."

She hated the little room they were standing in. She felt as if she couldn't breathe. She hated having to look at him and say goodbye.

"You ruined everything," she told him. "If you had just stayed away…"

"Then I would have missed my chance," he said, snatching up the handle of her suitcase and taking hold of her arm with his free hand.

"What're you doing?"

"Getting out of this bleeding closet for one," he told her. "We'll go outside to talk."

"No, we won't. I'm not going anywhere with you, Ronan." Laura dug in her heels and pulled back when he tugged at her.

"You'll come. Either under your own power or tossed over my shoulder. Your choice."

She looked up into his eyes and knew he wasn't kidding. So to spare herself the humiliation of being the center of attention at the airport, she gave in. When he opened the door, she sailed past Eddie and gave him a fierce frown when Ronan thanked the man for his help.

Laura's heels clicked against the linoleum floor. She heard the monotone voice coming over the speakers announcing flights she wouldn't be taking and she heard the whirr of her suitcase wheels as Ronan marched them straight through the doors into the cold Irish wind.

The roar of a jet taking off muffled his voice when he said, "This way," and gave her another tug.

Laura was still frowning when he drew her across the parking lot and stopped beside his shiny black Range Rover.

"Say what you have to say already," she told him. "I've still got time to catch another flight to Heathrow to make my connection."

Ronan looked down at her and felt his world wobble before steadying up. He'd spent the drive from Galway, figuring out what he wanted to say to her, but now that she was here, in front of him, his plan dried up and the words came tumbling out.

"You'd no right to leave me like that, Laura. Without so much as a word."

"I didn't do it to hurt you," she argued. "Or to make you mad. I was trying to make this easier on both of us."

"How could it ever be easy, losing you?"

"Ronan—"

"No," he cut her off fast and grabbed hold of her shoulders when she would have turned away. They were in a damned car park with the stench of cars all around them and the thunder of jets in the distance. Not the romantic scene he'd imagined, at the round tower behind the manor.

But the day a man told his woman he loved her carried its own beauty. One that could be found, he told himself, even in a car park. Taking a breath, he said, "You had your say in that bloody note. Now it's my turn."

Nodding, she pulled back from him, and his hands curled into empty fists without the touch of her.

"Fine," she said. "Say it then. Tell me how we should be married as friends."

"I love you."

She stopped. Blinked. Stared. "What?"

"Not the way I'd planned to say it, but you drive me to distraction, woman, so I'll say it again, just to make certain that you heard me." He grabbed hold of her and this time, she didn't pull away. Yanking her in close, he looked down into her blue eyes and lost himself there. "I *love* you, Laura."

"Ronan—"

"If you hadn't bloody well run off to the airport," he added, "I'd have told you all of this by the round tower. I had a plan."

"A plan?" A small smile curved her mouth.

"Aye. It came to me this morning—" He stopped and frowned. "*Before* Maeve showed up with that bleeding note." Scowling to himself, he hurried on. "I've been a fool."

"You have."

He snorted a laugh. "Figures that now you'd be agreeing with me."

She grabbed hold of the lapels of his suit and tugged. "Keep talking, Ronan. I'm listening."

"All right then, I'll lay it all at your feet and then you make your choice. A plane. Or home. With me."

Laura nodded, and the wind caught the ends of her hair, lifting it into a tangle about her face. Her smile was soft and understanding. Her eyes glimmered with a sheen of tears that he hoped to hell meant she was happy. He stared down at her and realized what he'd almost lost.

He sighed and said, "Once I thought that if I never said the word *love,* that I'd be safe. I'd keep from making the mistakes my parents had and wouldn't pay the price in misery. The truth is, I didn't want to love you, Laura."

She shook her head. "Liar."

Ronan grinned. "Aye, all right, that's a lie. I wanted to. I was just too—"

"Doesn't matter." She reached up and cupped his cheek in the palm of his hand, and he felt the soft, steady heat of her ease inside him.

He caught her hand in his and held it in place. "The truth is, without the word *love,* nothing is safe. Because nothing matters."

"I do love you," she whispered.

A car honked and someone shouted and Ronan grinned.

"I'll want to hear that often," he warned.

"Me, too," she said.

"I love you, Laura. And you'll be going nowhere this day or any other unless it's with me."

She laughed a little and shook her head. "I still have to go back, Ronan. I've got a home in California. A business."

"I've thought of that as well," he rushed on, refusing to accept any hindrances to the future he could see laying out in front of them. "If you want to sell real estate, you can do that here, you know. Or you could paint. You've a lovely gift for it, Laura, and I'd be proud to see you make something of it."

"Oh, Ronan—"

"As to your business," he said, "if you want to remain partners with Georgia, we can do that, too. I'll need to go back and forth to America on business. We can live half the year here and the other half there, if it suits you."

"I'll want to go back to visit," she said on a laugh, "but my home's here now. With you."

He grabbed her close, wrapped both arms around her and held on tightly. Ronan hadn't even realized just how worried he'd been that he'd waited too long to come to his senses. That she might not believe him when he told her he loved her. That she might not want to take the risk of loving him.

"That's grand, Laura," he murmured, into her hair, drawing the scent of her deep inside him, where it tangled in his blood and settled to stay.

After a long moment, when his heart eased into a steady beat, he drew her back from him, looked down at her and smiled. "I'll do this the proper way later, at the round tower. But for now, will you marry me, Laura? Will you stay with me and love me? Will you have children with me and build a home?"

Her smile was wide and bright as she said, "Yes, Ronan. I'll stay with you, and I will love you always."

"That might not be long enough," he whispered, dipping his head for a kiss.

Epilogue

The wedding was held a month later in Huntington Beach, California.

After the ceremony, a small reception was held at Laura's—now Georgia's—condo. The whole place had been decked out in ribbons and flowers. Music spilled from the stereo and the caterers were moving through the crowd, offering champagne.

Even Beast wore a wreath of daisies around his scruffy head, managing to look both offended and pleased with the situation.

Laura's parents had come down from Oregon for the wedding. Ronan had worried about meeting them, but he needn't have. They were, as Laura had assured him, lovely people. They'd welcomed him into their family and had already promised to join them for Christmas in Ireland.

Laura's business had taken a bit of doing to straighten

out, but that was done now as well, since she had signed over full interest to Georgia. In spite of her sister's objections, she'd deeded the condo to Georgia as well. The Page sisters had spent the last month laughing and crying and making plans for Georgia to come and stay in Dunley for a long visit.

Ronan's gaze swept the crowded room. Brian, his assistant, was chatting up a lovely redhead. Sam Travis and his wife were laughing with Laura's parents. There were friends, employees and family gathered together and Ronan gave silent thanks for every last one of them.

"You'll have to be married again in Ireland," Sean said, stepping up beside him and handing him a beer. "Everyone at home is upset they're missing the party."

"I know. I've already heard that Patsy is planning a celebration for when we get back." *We,* he thought with an inner smile. He and his wife would be going home after a weeklong stay at a private island in the Caribbean. Having Laura all to himself for a week of sun and sex sounded wonderful at the moment.

His life had become complete, all because of one stubborn woman with eyes as deep as the ocean and a heart truer than any he'd ever known.

"You'll get Beast back home?" Ronan asked. "The quarantine papers are filled out and—"

"Aye, you've told me," Sean said. "Not to worry. Beast will be there at the manor when you two get home."

Home sounded good to Ronan. Home with Laura sounded even better.

"The plane's fueled and ready to leave whenever you get to the airport," Sean said. "I've stocked the galley with champagne, as well."

"You're a good man, Sean," Ronan said on a grin.

Sean grinned right back at him. "And happy I am that it's *you* going off on a honeymoon and not me."

"I thought the same not so very long ago," Ronan reminded him.

"Ah, but your Laura's one of a kind, isn't she?"

"She is at that."

"Still, Georgia seems a likely lass. She's promised to show me the sights while I'm here."

Ronan sent his cousin a hard look. "That's Laura's sister there, Sean. Don't do something that would make me have to kill you."

Sean laughed. "Just a bit of fun is all, Ronan. Nothing to worry about I'm sure."

Ronan would have had more to say on the subject, but then his lovely bride came up to him and said, "Dance with me."

He handed his beer off to Sean and left his cousin without a backward glance.

"Have I told you, Mrs. Connolly, what a lovely bride you make?"

"You have, Mr. Connolly," she teased, moving into his arms as the crowd parted and began to applaud. "But it never hurts to hear it again."

"You're the loveliest thing I've ever seen," he said for her ears alone. "And I'm a damned lucky man."

"That you are," she agreed and smiled at him, her heart in her eyes.

The music soared, cheers erupted and even Beast howled his appreciation as the newlyweds kissed and sealed their future with a promise.

* * * * *

REQUEST YOUR FREE BOOKS!
2 FREE NOVELS PLUS 2 FREE GIFTS!

Harlequin® *Desire*

ALWAYS POWERFUL, PASSIONATE AND PROVOCATIVE

YES! Please send me 2 FREE Harlequin Desire® novels and my 2 FREE gifts (gifts are worth about $10). After receiving them, if I don't wish to receive any more books, I can return the shipping statement marked "cancel." If I don't cancel, I will receive 6 brand-new novels every month and be billed just $4.30 per book in the U.S. or $4.99 per book in Canada. That's a saving of at least 14% off the cover price! It's quite a bargain! Shipping and handling is just 50¢ per book in the U.S. and 75¢ per book in Canada.* I understand that accepting the 2 free books and gifts places me under no obligation to buy anything. I can always return a shipment and cancel at any time. Even if I never buy another book, the two free books and gifts are mine to keep forever.

225/326 HDN FEF3

Name _____ (PLEASE PRINT)

Address _____ Apt. #

City _____ State/Prov. _____ Zip/Postal Code

Signature (if under 18, a parent or guardian must sign)

Mail to the **Reader Service:**

IN U.S.A.: P.O. Box 1867, Buffalo, NY 14240-1867
IN CANADA: P.O. Box 609, Fort Erie, Ontario L2A 5X3

Not valid for current subscribers to Harlequin Desire books.

Want to try two free books from another line?
Call 1-800-873-8635 or visit www.ReaderService.com.

* Terms and prices subject to change without notice. Prices do not include applicable taxes. Sales tax applicable in N.Y. Canadian residents will be charged applicable taxes. Offer not valid in Quebec. This offer is limited to one order per household. All orders subject to credit approval. Credit or debit balances in a customer's account(s) may be offset by any other outstanding balance owed by or to the customer. Please allow 4 to 6 weeks for delivery. Offer available while quantities last.

Your Privacy—The Reader Service is committed to protecting your privacy. Our Privacy Policy is available online at www.ReaderService.com or upon request from the Reader Service.

We make a portion of our mailing list available to reputable third parties that offer products we believe may interest you. If you prefer that we not exchange your name with third parties, or if you wish to clarify or modify your communication preferences, please visit us at www.ReaderService.com/consumerschoice or write to us at Reader Service Preference Service, P.O. Box 9062, Buffalo, NY 14269. Include your complete name and address.

HDES11B

HARLEQUIN® Blaze™
red-hot reads

Two sizzling fairy tales with men straight from your wildest dreams...

Fan-favorite authors

Rhonda Nelson & Karen Foley

bring readers another installment of

Blazing Bedtime Stories, Volume IX

THE EQUALIZER

Modern-day righter of wrongs, Robin Sherwood is a man on a mission and will do everything necessary to see that through, especially when that means catching the eye of a fair maiden.

GOD'S GIFT TO WOMEN

Sculptor Lexi Adams decides there is no such thing as the perfect man, until she catches sight of Nikos Christakos, the sexy builder next door. She convinces herself that she only wants to sculpt him, but soon finds a cold stone statue is a poor substitute for the real deal.

Available October 2012 wherever books are sold.

New York Times *bestselling author Brenda Jackson presents TEXAS WILD, a brand-new Westmoreland novel.*

Available October 2012 from Harlequin Desire®!

Rico figured there were a lot of things in life he didn't know. But the one thing he did know was that there was no way Megan Westmoreland was going to Texas with him. He was attracted to her, big-time, and had been from the moment he'd seen her at Micah's wedding four months ago. Being alone with her in her office was bad enough. But the idea of them sitting together on a plane or in a car was arousing him just thinking about it.

He could tell by the mutinous expression on her face that he was in for a fight. That didn't bother him. Growing up, he'd had two younger sisters to deal with, so he knew well how to handle a stubborn female.

She crossed her arms over her chest. "Other than the fact that you prefer working alone, give me another reason I can't go with you."

He crossed his arms over his own chest. "I don't need another reason. You and I talked before I took this case, and I told you I would get you the information you wanted… doing things my way."

He watched as she nibbled on her bottom lip. So now she was remembering. Good. Even so, he couldn't stop looking into her beautiful dark eyes, meeting her fiery gaze head-on.

"As the client, I demand that you take me," she said.

He narrowed his gaze. "You can demand all you want, but you're not going to Texas with me."

Megan's jaw dropped. "I *will* be going with you since there's no good reason that I shouldn't."

He didn't say anything for a moment. "Okay, there is another reason I won't take you with me. One that you'd do well to consider," he said in a barely controlled tone. She had pushed him, and he didn't like being pushed.

"Fine, let's hear it," she snapped furiously.

He placed his hands in the pockets of his jeans, stood with his legs braced apart and leveled his gaze on her. "I want you, Megan. Bad. And if you go anywhere with me, I'm going to have you."

He then turned and walked out of her office.

Will Megan go to Texas with Rico?

Find out in Brenda Jackson's brand-new Westmoreland novel, TEXAS WILD.

Available October 2012 from Harlequin Desire®.